Sewing & Mending Cottage

De-ann Black

Text copyright © 2024 by De-ann Black
Cover Design & Illustration © 2024 by De-ann Black

All rights reserved.
No part of this book may be used or reproduced in any manner whatsoever without the written consent of the author.

This is a work of fiction. Names, characters, places, and incidents are either products of the author's imagination or are used fictitiously. Any resemblance to actual persons, living or dead, businesses, companies, events, or locales is entirely coincidental.

Paperback edition published 2024

Sewing & Mending Cottage

ISBN: 9798880258918

Sewing & Mending Cottage is the first book in the Scottish Loch Romance series.

1. Sewing & Mending Cottage
2. Scottish Loch Summer Romance
3. Sweet Music

Also by De-ann Black (Romance, Action/Thrillers & Children's books). See her Amazon Author page or website for further details about her books, screenplays, illustrations and artwork. www.De-annBlack.com

Action/Thrillers:
Knight in Miami.
Agency Agenda.
Love Him Forever.
Someone Worse.
Electric Shadows.
The Strife of Riley.
Shadows of Murder.

Romance:
Sweet Music
Love & Lyrics
Christmas Weddings
Fairytale Christmas on the Island
The Cure for Love at Christmas
Vintage Dress Shop on the Island
Scottish Island Fairytale Castle
Scottish Loch Summer Romance
Scottish Island Knitting Bee
Sewing & Mending Cottage
Knitting Shop by the Sea
Colouring Book Cottage
Knitting Cottage
Oops! I'm the Paparazzi, Again
The Bitch-Proof Wedding
Embroidery Cottage
The Dressmaker's Cottage
The Sewing Shop
Heather Park
The Tea Shop by the Sea
The Bookshop by the Seaside

The Sewing Bee
The Quilting Bee
Snow Bells Wedding
Snow Bells Christmas
Summer Sewing Bee
The Chocolatier's Cottage
Christmas Cake Chateau
The Beemaster's Cottage
The Sewing Bee By The Sea
The Flower Hunter's Cottage
The Christmas Knitting Bee
The Sewing Bee & Afternoon Tea
Shed In The City
The Bakery By The Seaside
The Christmas Chocolatier
The Christmas Tea Shop & Bakery
The Bitch-Proof Suit

Colouring books:
Summer Nature. Flower Nature. Summer Garden. Spring Garden. Autumn Garden. Sea Dream. Festive Christmas. Christmas Garden. Flower Bee. Wild Garden. Flower Hunter. Stargazer Space. Christmas Theme. Faerie Garden Spring. Scottish Garden Seasons. Bee Garden.

Embroidery books:
Floral Garden Embroidery Patterns
Floral Spring Embroidery Patterns
Christmas & Winter Embroidery Patterns
Floral Nature Embroidery Designs
Scottish Garden Embroidery Designs

Contents

Chapter One	1
Chapter Two	16
Chapter Three	29
Chapter Four	42
Chapter Five	55
Chapter Six	71
Chapter Seven	83
Chapter Eight	97
Chapter Nine	111
Chapter Ten	125
Chapter Eleven	138
Chapter Twelve	154
About De-ann Black	177

CHAPTER ONE

There she was, all lit up in the window of her cottage, busy sewing into the night. Penny's white–painted cottage was set on the hillside overlooking the loch with the vast star–studded sky arching above the surrounding fields in the heart of the Scottish Highlands.

Lamps from the nearby village main street shone like twinkle lights. The shops were closed for the evening, and were barely a two minute walk away. Everything blended into a picturesque niche of cottages sprinkled like sweets on the rolling hillside, a cosy community of shops — including a grocery shop, bakery, tiny post office, quilt shop and crafters, sweet shop and florist.

Gaven hadn't met Penny since she'd arrived to set up her sewing and mending business in the cottage near the loch, but he'd read her website and felt that he knew a little bit about her. And there was the gossip in the small, friendly community. He'd heard plenty of talk about Penny making a big, bold move — leaving her life in the city behind, in Glasgow, and setting up home in the cosy cottage in the Highlands.

He admired her for taking a chance on a fresh start. Apparently, she'd worked as a designer and pattern cutter for a fashion company for several years. Recently, the company was bought over and she'd been made redundant, but had used the redundancy money to secure a mortgage on the cottage rather than save it for a rainy day and find alternative work in the city.

The fashion company job had never been Penny's dream job. She'd always wanted to have her own sewing and mending business and had worked from home in the evenings while employed by the fashion company. Now, circumstances had led to her forging out on her own, according to the gossip.

In her early thirties she was the same age as him. And very pretty. And single. Not that he planned to get involved with her. He was too busy, and romance never went well for him.

Since she'd moved to the cottage early in January, he'd been away a lot on business, but in the past week when he went for his evening run he'd seen the windows of her cottage aglow late at night as she worked on repairing clothes and making them wearable again.

Apparently, her creative mending skills were excellent and she'd recently been featured in sewing and craft magazines. Her website stated that she did do invisible mending on garments. But where she excelled, and what she was becoming known for in crafting circles, was *visible mending* — using bright coloured thread and embroidery motifs and various stitching techniques to mend a tear or worn fabric on jeans, jackets, skirts, dresses, all sorts of items. She was skilled at embroidery and coupled with her fashion, design and artistic talent, she made the repairs a design feature of the garments.

Darning, appliqué and quilting, including using hexies as patchwork repairs, were part of her methods.

Saving well–loved but well–worn garments from being cast aside, finding thrifty vintage buys to reinvent, and breathing new life into long forgotten items hanging in the wardrobe and upgrading them with thread, yarn, ribbon and fabric scraps was exciting. She loved personalising clothing and made mending sound like fun.

As someone with zero talent for sewing, and never having stitched anything, not even a shirt button, he'd poured over the information on her website with interest, and she'd become the stranger he felt he knew quite well.

He was bound to meet her properly soon now that he was back home, living in his castle on his estate. Business often took him away to the cities, Glasgow, Edinburgh and London throughout the year, but the money he made from his investments kept his estate financially stable. Unlike his private life, a small, ever changing chain of romantic disasters. But at least the estate was solvent, and as he was responsible for the upkeep of it, that others depended on too, the wealth he'd inherited and accumulated through his own hard work and merit, far outweighed not having someone, a girlfriend, hopefully one day a wife, to share it with.

Pausing at the edge of the loch for a moment to glance over at Penny's cottage, he then sprinted on, running through the night, keeping himself fit and enjoying the excitement he felt every time he ran there, feeling free and light from the responsibilities that weighed heavily on his shoulders during the daylight hours.

There he was, that tall, broad shouldered, manly silhouette, dressed in dark coloured fitness gear, lit up against the shimmering light from the loch.

Penny didn't know him, but he intrigued her. These past few nights he'd raced along the edge of the loch before doubling back and powering through the night. Whatever was spurring him on, she could only guess at.

Maybe she'd ask the ladies at the crafting bee night. A note had been popped through her door inviting her to join them. The bee night was held in the laird's castle, a castle that she'd seen from a distance. It looked impressive and was available for hire for special occasions like weddings and parties. She'd skimmed the castle's website and seen that it offered special stays for guests such as authors seeking a writing retreat, artists and creatives looking for somewhere to relax. Lodges within the castle grounds provided self catering retreats. It appeared to be invariably fully booked.

She'd never met the laird and heard that he was often away on business, working on financial dealings in the city that helped keep the estate afloat. She pictured him as a well–dressed, older gentleman, grumpy and standoffish.

The crafting bee nights were held once a week in the castle's function room. The bee nights finished through Christmas and New Year, and resumed again in late January.

Penny had arrived at the cottage early in January and was still getting to know everyone in the village, so when the invitation to join the crafting bee popped through her letterbox, she was happy to be part of it. Another tick box on the fresh start she'd hoped for. She was looking forward to an evening of sewing, quilting, dressmaking, knitting and all sorts of crafts. Mending was what she intended working on and was keen to see what the other members were making.

Sitting beside the living room window, she finished sewing the embroidered floral motif on a denim jacket and closed her sewing basket for the night.

Hanging up the jacket on the rail of garments at the far end of the living room where her sewing machine was set up, she decided to step outside and breathe in the fresh air before getting ready for bed. It would help her sleep. She wouldn't settle easily after sewing for the entire evening, even if she loved her sewing, embroidery and repair stitching more than anything. It was still long hours worked from the twilight's glow to midnight and later, like this evening.

The long living room stretched from the front window to the back of the cottage with a view of the garden. The snow had melted as January came to a close and snowdrops were making an appearance. Her small garden was sparse of flowers except for the hardy little white and green snowdrops. But she'd noticed that lilac, yellow and purple crocus and winter pansies were sprouting up in other cottage gardens. She hoped to sketch some of them for her embroidery designs.

The real log fire had almost burned itself out, rather like she had, so she went through to the hall and opened the front door with the intention of a quick breath of air before bedtime.

She wore a soft white jumper she'd knitted herself and jeans duly patched with the ubiquitous colourful embroidery stitching she was becoming synonymous with. Her slipper boots would suffice to stand outside the cottage and breathe in the brisk night air.

There was a hint of frost in the air, adding to the crispness she'd come to enjoy in the quiet of the night after a long day of creative mending.

The darkness was never as deep as she would've imagined. The loch bore a shimmer, even on stormy nights, and the rolling hills and countryside beyond allowed the vast arching sky, glittering with stars, to cast a luminous glow across the scenery.

There was never anyone around except...the elusive runner, a recent addition to her world. Her pale grey eyes peered into the night. He'd disappeared into the shadows further along the loch, so she had it all to herself. Sheer bliss. She didn't miss the city for a second.

Taking a deep breath, she felt herself relax while admiring the stars, so clear in the night sky. Maybe one day she'd take an interest in what the constellations were, but for now, they were beautiful. In the city, the stars were scarce twinkles on a clear night, but nothing like this magnificent view.

She took another deep breath, feeling a sudden breeze blow through her silky, shoulder length blonde hair.

And then...

Click.

Penny glanced over her shoulder. 'Nooo!' The front door had blown shut.

She hurried over hoping she'd remembered to keep the latch on, but no, tiredness had made her leave it easy to close. And it had.

She placed her hands on her slim waist and tried not to panic. She was locked out of her cottage. There had to be one window that she hadn't snibbed.

Pulling at the living room window where she'd been sitting sewing, proved futile. It was shut tight.

The kitchen! Filled with a sudden burst of enthusiasm that she was bound to have left that window open when she was making dinner, she rushed round to the back of the cottage and found it was shut as tightly as the living room. No joy from the bathroom at the back either.

Trailing round to the front of the cottage again, she wondered if her slipper boots could tackle the terrain if she had to walk to the village's main street to ask for help, as her phone was inside the cottage, so she'd no way to contact anyone. Not that she had anyone's number to phone, but still...

What was Penny doing standing outside her cottage at this time of night? She looked cold, unless wrapping her arms around herself was a habit.

Gaven ran back along the edge of the loch, watching her. The white jumper and light blonde hair stood out against the shadows, and he could see her fairly clearly against the white painted backdrop of the cottage.

She seemed...perturbed.

Should he offer to help her? Was she in need of his assistance? Or would this be the wrong time to approach her, to meet her for the first time? First impressions and all that. Not that he intended making a great first impression. Okay, that was a lie. He wanted to make a good first impression, but he didn't want to think why this seemed so necessary.

He paused and watched her...what was she doing? Trying to climb in the window of her cottage? Or was it some sort of exercise routine? She stood near one of the front windows, the bedroom window and was reaching up, and then flopping down again. Very strange. Very, very strange behaviour. But she was a city girl. There was no accounting for what type of things she considered acceptable.

Oh, no. Now she was trying to climb up on the window ledge. It wasn't high, but she seemed to be wearing furry slipper boots.

He had to take a chance and risk looking like a fool as he raced up the hill towards her cottage.

Penny heard someone running towards her, and blinked when she saw it was *him*.

Was he coming to help her? The handsome night runner to the rescue?

He looked strong, and lean and fit in his training gear and T–shirt and...she was all alone...

No, don't think about that. The local gossip never mentioned anything about anyone being pounced on when they were all alone on a dark night in the middle of the Highlands with only the light from the cottage and glimmer from the loch to illuminate them.

She was petite and he was tall, strong and could overpower her, but she'd put up a fight. If it came to that. She'd spring on him and take him by surprise. No way was she going quietly into the night. He'd have a wildcat on his hands.

She could run too. Slipper boots or not. And she was faaaast! She'd always been a fast runner.

'Are you okay?' he shouted as he approached, trying to assure her that he wasn't aiming to body tackle her down on to the grass and have his wicked way with her. There was a wary glint in her eyes coupled with a warning.

'Yes, no,' she replied.

This was going to be complicated. He could tell.

'I've locked myself out.'

Her lovely grey eyes were wide with trepidation. She looked exactly like the pictures on her website. And the videos. She made videos to demonstrate her repair it and wear it sewing techniques. But even though she was a familiar stranger, of sorts, his heart was beating fast and strong, and the instinct to protect her washed over him, along with the desire to assure her he wasn't an untrustworthy rotter, or whatever that accusatory look was in her eyes.

He noticed that she barely came up to his shoulders. She was petite but with a feisty glint in her eyes, as if she was prepared to wrestle him if he stepped out of line.

'You're quite safe,' he said. 'I've no intention of compromising you, Penny.'

He knew her name! She stared at him, taken aback. She didn't know his name.

He got the look and gestured around the area where her cottage was perched halfway up the gently rolling hillside that led down to the shore of the loch. 'This is part of my castle's estate.'

'You're the grumpy, standoffish laird?' The words were out before she could stop them. She blamed the situation and the effect he was having on her. Raw masculinity at this proximity, at this time of night, under the current circumstances were to blame for her outburst.

Gaven swallowed the unintentional, he was sure, insult.

He nodded and stepped forward. 'Let me try to open the window.'

She stepped aside and watched the muscles in his arms tense as he pushed up on the window, easing it open enough for her to crawl through.

'Want a lift up?' he offered, seeing her getting ready to launch herself at the gap he'd made.

'No...' She attempted to climb over the snowdrops around the edge of the cottage garden. 'Yes,' she said, unable to do so without flattening the snowdrops that had punched through the winter ground to help announce the arrival of spring.

He lifted her up as if she was a lightweight broom, and turned her like an arrow aiming to post her through the window gap.

'Hold on a minute,' she said. 'I don't even know your name.'

'Gaven,' he said, notching this up as the strangest introduction he'd ever made. Perhaps he'd made an impression after all. Good or bad? He wasn't sure. But it was definitely noteworthy.

As he helped to post her through the gap he tried not to grab hold of her thighs, but this proved difficult as she was worried he'd drop her.

'Don't drop me,' she told him.

'I won't. I've got a firm grip of you.'

'I'm going to try to bounce on to the bed,' she announced.

'No, it's too far, you'll tumble. Just ease yourself in gently.'

She wriggled and one of her slippers fell off.

He noticed that the heel of her sock had been mended with brightly coloured thread.

'That's a very nice piece of mending on your sock,' he said.

'Thank you. I used different colours of thread.'

'I'm going to lean in and lower you into the bedroom.' Without pausing for her consent, he did just that.

'Great! I'm in,' she announced, scrambling up from the floor. 'That was awkward.'

Then she disappeared and he heard the front door open. She stood there smiling and looking pink cheeked and startled, but happy.

'Here's your slipper.'

She put it on.

The heat from the cottage poured out but she welcomed the warmth, along with the delicious aroma of ginger and cinnamon. She liked to bake and had made a gingerbread cake for dinner.

'I enjoy baking,' she explained noticing the scent of her home baking register with him.

'I can't cook for toffee,' he revealed.

She supposed he'd have staff to do the cooking and tending to guests at the castle.

He glanced over her shoulder, not from angling for an invitation to come in, merely curious about her and if she'd settled in. He noticed a pile of folded pieces of various colours and prints of fabric on the hall table and surmised these were used for her repairs.

A warm jacket and scarf were hanging from a hook. Her trademark patches and embroidery stitching were evident on both. She'd have benefited from wearing them when she'd stepped out of her cottage for a late night breath of air, but he didn't want to tell her in case it sounded like scolding.

'I take it you've settled in well,' he said, filling the void of silence.

'Yes, the cottage is perfect. Everything I'd hoped for.'

'Not missing the city then?'

'Not at all.'

'I'm not long back from a business trip to the cities. But I'm always glad to be home.'

Home? Could a castle feel like home she wondered.

He'd seen that look so many times over the years and answered her unspoken question. 'I was brought up in the castle, so it's home to me, though I know others may think that a cottage like this is cosier.'

'Home is where the heart is and all that.' She tried to sound chipper, when she sensed that their conversation was mildly unnerving. He certainly disconcerted her. A laird. A real, Scottish laird, was standing on her doorstep chatting in the depths of the night. While he was dressed like a proverbial athlete. There was that aspect to contend with. He. Was. Handsome. Imposing in stature, with a shock of rich, auburn hair and eyes that were grey–green with dark lashes. Those eyes looked at her with an intelligence bordering on scrutiny, but as he was still lingering on her doorstep exchanging pleasantries she thought she must have passed muster.

'I thought we'd meet soon,' he confessed. 'Not quite in such unusual circumstances, but I would've called to introduce myself. But I've been exceedingly busy. The New Year is always hectic before settling down in the spring. Summer is wonderfully chaotic, then there's the mellowness of autumn before the hectic Christmas celebrations.'

Penny found herself laughing.

Those eyes of his looked at her and he tilted his head and frowned.

'Sorry, you sound perpetually busy.'

He released a smile. 'Yes, I suppose I am.'

'You need to make time to enjoy yourself,' she told him firmly.

His expression showed mild surprise. He clearly wasn't used to being given advice and certainly not from a newcomer. But perhaps that was better. The observations of someone unfamiliar with the village might have a clearer view.

'I'll keep that in mind,' he promised.

She wondered if he would.

'As laird, it's my responsibility to oversee the running of things in the community. To ensure that everything works as well as possible, that people have support when needed from myself and other members of the community, and that life is made to benefit those living here.'

Not one flicker of false words or well–meaning exaggeration showed on his face. The laird clearly took his responsibilities seriously. Something that did show in the depths of his grey–green eyes, an inner strength that she found herself appreciating.

'I've seen your website,' he told her.

It was a throwaway comment she grabbed with interest. Her mind raced through the main features on her website, picturing what he'd seen, the impression of her he'd gleaned from it.

'I've had a peek at the castle's hotel facilities,' she countered. 'The crafting bee nights are starting again there and I've been invited to join them.' Her tone indicated that this was her excuse for looking at his website.

'The bee nights are popular. Tea, cake and shortbread galore. And sewing, quilting, knitting, and I now presume creative mending.'

'Yes, that's my plan.'

He took a deep breath. 'Well, I'd better get going.'

'Thank you for coming to my rescue.'

He nodded, smiled and started to walk away.

'I'm sorry I insulted you, Gaven,' she called after him.

'Think nothing of it, Penny. Good–night.' His rich as malt whisky voice sounded clear in the crisp air.

She closed the door, hurried through to the bedroom, and without putting the light on she peered out and watched him run away into the night.

Gaven the laird had impressed her, disconcerted her and intrigued her. Three reasons to beware. Her heart could be in jeopardy.

CHAPTER TWO

Penny walked to the shops the next morning for fresh bread and milk. She didn't even have enough milk for a cuppa, so popping out to the shops was a priority. Her blonde hair was freshly washed and dried, and she wore a pastel pink jumper with her jeans, and the embroidery adorned denim jacket that had been hanging up in the hall.

Pale sunlight brightened the day. The lilac, white and purple heather on the hills looked like a natural patchwork against the greenery. The loch had a stillness to it, and reflected the blue sky on its calm surface.

She had to pass by a few cottages, including one that had a garden filled with early flourishing spring flowers. She hadn't yet met all her nearest neighbours, through circumstances and being so busy settling in and forging on with her business. She'd never met the owner of this lovely cottage, whitewashed like hers, but with a low fence around the garden and a front door that was open to the world.

Slowing down so that she could peek at the petals of the pansies and crocus, she suddenly realised that the owner, a man, tall and distinguished looking, was now standing in the doorway watching her. In his mid thirties, and classically dressed in well–cut dark trousers and an open neck white shirt, he had a cooking utensil in one hand and a casual expression on his face.

'Pick any flowers you want,' he offered in a voice that sounded deep and smooth.

Penny stood up from peering at his flowers and smiled tightly.

'I was just looking at them, at the colours and counting the petals,' she explained. This probably didn't explain anything he wanted to know and appeared to pique his interest in her.

'If it's for your sewing patterns, your embroidery designs, do help yourself, Penny.'

The sound of her name on his firm but smiling lips caused her heart to flutter with unexpected excitement. His features were classically handsome, and even from this distance she could see that his eyes were a stunning pale aqua blue. His light brown hair was well–cut, and he had a businessman air about him, and yet...there was a lot more to him.

Working in fashion in the city, she'd met plenty of business types, money men, interested in finance rather than fashion even though they sometimes invested in it. Yes, she'd met them over the years. This man, standing on his cottage doorstep, looking like he belonged somewhere else entirely, wasn't one of those types. She could often suss someone out from the clothes they wore. Call it a knack, a quirk, an ability gleaned from her interest in clothing since she was a young girl. But he was a bit of a mystery. Perhaps the cooking spoon indicated that he was a chef. No, he didn't fit that mould either.

'Yes, it is for my embroidery designs. I'm planning to sketch spring flowers for my new patterns,' she told him.

Something sounded in his kitchen causing him to hurry inside. He beckoned her to come in.

'I've got the pan ready to cook Scotch pancakes for breakfast,' he said, striding ahead of her.

Feeling intrigued and obviously welcome, she followed him inside, leaving the front door wide open. The appetising aroma of fresh baked Scotch pancakes, drop scones, filled the traditionally furnished cottage. He'd cooked two to test the temperature and consistency, and a couple of tasty looking pancakes sat on a plate on the kitchen table while the kettle boiled.

Penny hadn't yet eaten breakfast and she hoped the low rumble in her tummy was inaudible above his bustling around.

He busied himself in the kitchen, checking the frying pan on the top of the stove was hot and ready for the mixture he'd made from flour, eggs and whatever else he'd added, to be poured on and cooked.

'I've a book of flower photographs that you may find handy,' he said, pointing to a book tucked up on one of the kitchen shelves. 'That one up there with the vintage botanical cover.'

Penny lifted the book down and opened it to reveal a wonderfully artistic journal filled with photos of flowers that appeared to have been taken in his garden. She recognised the fence and there were glimpses of the cottage in the background. He'd stuck the pictures into the blank pages and added notes, the names of the flowers and when they'd blossomed. Rough notes, but handy information.

'Are these yours?' She sounded impressed. The close–up pictures were particularly interesting, and her mind was already thinking how useful this would be to give her an accurate base on which to sketch her floral designs for embroidering.

'Yes, I've been taking pictures of the garden for the past year, since I first arrived. I use them for my work, but we're in different businesses. We won't clash on designs.'

'I'm afraid I don't know your name or your business.'

'Neil. Goldsmith and jeweller.'

Now the pieces of his attire, confident manner and lovely cottage started to fit together. There were artistic pictures of engagements rings and wedding rings set amid the flowers, taken in close–up, showing the beauty of the gold and diamond jewellery in the floral setting.

'The pictures of your jewellery with the flowers are gorgeous,' she said, admiring them.

'I put them on my website to promote the jewellery. The flowers seemed like a suitable background for the engagement and wedding rings.'

By now he was trying to juggle making the pancakes and the tea.

'Want a hand?' she offered.

'The kettle's boiled. Could you make us a pot of tea?' He glanced at the ceramic teapot and mugs on hooks on the beautiful wooden dresser. 'Teabags are in the pot.'

Putting the book down out of harm's way, she filled the teapot with the boiling water, gave it a stir, put the lid on and sat it on the kitchen table. A plate was set for one.

'Help yourself to a plate,' he said, scooping the next batch of pancakes over to cook nicely on the flip side. 'Cutlery is in the dresser drawer.'

Okay, she thought. If he was offering flower photos and breakfast, she wasn't going to be silly and refuse just because she'd never met him. The pancakes looked and smelled sooo tasty.

Setting a plate and cutlery for herself at the table, she watched as he piled four pancakes on to her plate.

'Four?' She looked at him, wondering if she should divide them between the two plates.

But no, four for her and the next batch were for him. She supposed they'd draw straws for the two he'd already cooked. Or maybe it would be one each, or she'd take a couple home to eat in the afternoon.

'The milk is in the fridge,' he told her. 'I take my tea strong, a splash of milk and no sugar.'

'Same as me. Two teas coming up.' This time she sounded genuinely chipper and felt quite happy to have breakfast with a handsome stranger. There could be worse ways to start her day, including having to go to the shops and then traipse back to her cottage to cook something for herself. Neil's offer appealed to her. Probably later she'd realise that she shouldn't have overstepped the mark and propriety. Right now, all that was on her mind was how tasty breakfast looked.

Neil reached into the cupboard and brought out two jars of jam, strawberry and bramble, and a jar of local heather honey. He put them on the table and then opened the fridge.

'Butter?' he said.

'Yes please.' Melting butter on hot pancakes. Oh yes, she was up for that.

He put the butter dish down and she helped herself.

He took a sip of tea and encouraged her to try the jam or honey. 'The jam is locally made. And we've a beemaster. His heather honey is delicious.'

Four pancakes. Hmmm, she pondered. One with butter, one with butter and strawberry jam, one with just bramble jam and the last one with honey.

Neil started to tuck into his pancakes, buttering all of them and then adding honey to two. 'The butter is incredible, locally made too from the buttery.'

Penny cut a chunk of buttered pancake and popped it in her mouth. 'Mmmm,' she muttered.

'One of the perks of living here. Lots of local delicacies. But I'm sure you know this. You've been here now what...almost a month?'

She nodded, now eating another chunk of pancake.

He continued to eat his breakfast as he spoke to her. 'I've been meaning to pop round and introduce myself, but you always seem to be so busy with your sewing. You sit at that window stitching for long hours. I couldn't bring myself to interrupt.'

'I suppose you've seen my website.'

He shook his head. 'No, just heard the local chit-chat about you arriving and setting up your sewing and mending shop in the cottage.'

Penny considered this for a moment. 'I suppose it is a shop of sorts,' she mused. 'Maybe I should call it Sewing and Mending Cottage?'

'Don't let me influence your business plans. I don't always get my own marketing right.' He gestured towards the book. 'The flower and ring photos worked too well. I was inundated with orders. I'm only just catching up with the overspill. I'm a niche market. I mainly create custom designs for special customers. I'm used to taking my time with each piece rather than working on rush jobs. But I didn't want to let anyone down. It's my own fault for not considering this. I've ended the promotion now.'

'Apart from engagement and wedding rings, what type of jewellery do you make?'

'You haven't seen my website then either?'

'No. I've only looked at a few of the local shops' websites, especially the quilting and crafting ones. Oh, and I did check Gaven's castle website.'

'Have you met him?'

'Yes, late last night.' She explained the fiasco.

'If you're ever in a dilemma like that again, chap my door.'

'Thanks.'

'What did you make of our laird?'

'I had completely the wrong impression of him.'

'Did you think he'd be an older boy, a bit stuffy and standoffish?'

'Yes, something like that. But he was very helpful, even after I insulted him horribly.' She told him the details.

Neil laughed and then cupped his tea. His stunning aqua eyes looked at her across the kitchen table. 'Did he take it on the chin?'

'He did. I was impressed.'

Neil smiled. 'More fodder for the gossipmongers. Well meaning ones of course. And I'm sure that being insulted straight to his face was a new experience for Gaven.'

'I was tired. I'd been stitching into the twilight hours, then locked myself out of the cottage. I blurted out what was going through my mind. Something I do when I'm overworked and stressed.'

'I'm duly warned.'

'I wasn't meaning—'

But he was smiling, lightly teasing her, and then sipped his tea before topping up both their cups.

They were quiet for a moment, eating their pancakes as if they'd known each other longer and were content together.

That didn't mean her heart was calm. Quite the opposite. Neil was extremely attractive and something about him, a warmth, a calm assurance excited her. His hands were elegant but strong. And those stunning blue eyes of his. Wow!

'Penny for them, Penny.' He laughed. 'I'll bet you haven't heard that one before.'

'No marks for that one, Neil.'

Neil. He liked the way his name sounded when she said it. But he had no intention of letting himself become attracted to her. She was beautiful. So fresh and full of natural beauty and willingness to grasp a situation and enjoy it for what it was worth.

'Do you always eat a cooked breakfast like this?' she asked him.

'No, but I mended a gold bracelet for one of the farmers. It was his wife's favourite and the catch was damaged. I repaired it and didn't charge him anything. It didn't take me long and...' He shrugged. 'Anyway, the farmer dropped off a box of fresh eggs for me this morning, by way of thanks, so I thought — pancakes for breakfast and cheese soufflé for dinner.'

'What? No eggy pudding for lunch?'

'Don't encourage me.' He smiled, and she felt her heart react. For such a classically handsome man, he had such a sexy smile.

'I'm working through lunch today, as usual. I'm making an engagement and wedding ring for a top client.' He gestured to the book. 'They want a rose design engraved on the wedding ring. The rose is designed from one of photos.'

She reached for the book, having finished her pancakes and started to look through it. 'There are so many beautiful flower photos.'

'That's the rose there.' He pointed to it. A perfect white rose. 'I've sketched the design I'll engrave on the ring, so you can take the book away with you and use it for your embroidery patterns.'

'The pansies are especially handy. I'm working on pansy patterns later today. I should be working on them now, but someone waylaid me, tempting me into his cottage with a home cooked breakfast.'

'What a monster.'

She laughed. 'Speaking of monsters, I have to ask...is there one rumoured to be in the loch?'

'No, but you never know.'

'Don't say that!' she scolded him. 'I'll be wary now to go for a run at night.'

'With Gaven? Has he invited you to run with him?'

'No. I like to run, though I haven't done it in ages. City running isn't the same. Now that I have the perfect running spot outside my door, I thought I'd take advantage of it.'

'I'm not a runner myself. But I enjoy hillwalking, venturing out into the wilds. And I plan to head to the coast in the summer to swim. The cove isn't far. That's what I love about living here — heather covered hills, lush farmlands, mountains and the sea, and the cove only a short drive away.'

'It's idyllic, isn't it?'

'Yes, so I hope you'll enjoy living here, Penny.'

A surge of excitement charged through her looking at him smiling at her. Her heart fluttered and a blush started to form on her cheeks. She found Neil very handsome, classy and sexy. He could cook pancakes, and make her laugh at the same time. More dangerous territory.

What a predicament for her heart to be in. She'd just wanted to get on with her sewing and mending. But maybe it would be nice to be friends with Neil. Just friends.

'I'm not entirely sure what a goldsmith does to make jewellery,' she said as they finished breakfast and she got ready to leave, taking the book with her.

He gestured to his workshop that extended from a spare room into the back garden from the rear of the cottage. 'Want a peek?'

She did, and followed him through.

His workshop was light and airy and was equipped with his traditional workbench and tables that held the tools he used. Cutting tools and gadgets sat on the tables and it was far more artistic than she'd imagined. The large window let in the daylight and offered a view of the back garden where more flowers grew. Lamps provided extra lighting over specific workbench areas, and shelves were stacked with boxes and glass jars filled with findings and bits and pieces. A small safe was tucked unobtrusively under a bench, where he presumably kept valuable items.

'I cut, file and hammer the gold,' he explained, showing her around.

She barely came up to his shoulders. He was so tall and lean with broad shoulders. She couldn't help feeling attracted to him. Pushing these thoughts aside, she concentrated on what he was telling her about his work.

'I make rings, bracelets, necklaces and brooches. Some are set with precious and semi–precious gemstones. Wedding, anniversary and engagement rings are my top sellers.'

He lifted a piece of gold from one of the trays and handed it to her. 'I've always loved the lustre and feel of gold. It's wonderful to work with.'

'I've never held a piece of gold like this,' she said, admiring it, imagining what he'd make with it. She handed it back, and their hands accidentally brushed against each other. A frisson shot through her, and she pulled her hand away as if she'd been touched by a spark of fire. A blush formed across her cheeks and she stepped aside, taking an interest in the precious and semi–precious gems he'd been working with.

'Is that a light blue sapphire?' she asked him, leaning down and gazing at the gorgeous colour.

'Yes. The engagement ring I'm making has diamonds and sapphires set in yellow gold.'

He lifted another piece of gold that looked more like silver or platinum. 'This is a piece of white gold for another ring, a diamond cluster.'

She felt the texture and loved seeing all these precious elements, but when she handed it back to him she was careful not to brush those long, elegant fingers of his.

He was careful too.

So much for not letting himself become attracted to Penny, he thought. That plan was never going to work. He liked her. He liked her from the first moment he'd met her. There was a kindness and warmth that he felt from her that added to her beauty. He hadn't felt like this in a long time. But no doubt Gaven was interested in Penny. The way she'd described what had happened the previous night made him wonder if she was keen on getting to know the laird.

But maybe he could be friends with Penny.

She peered at bands of gold that would be made into exclusive wedding rings.

'These are some of the wedding rings I'm creating, with comfort in mind, the edges well–rounded inside and outside the band.' He glanced at her ring finger as if sizing it up in a second and then picked up one of the gold bands. 'Try it on.'

He handed her the ring and she slipped it on her finger. It was an ideal fit.

She held her hand out to admire it, seeing the gold lustre under one of the overhead lamps and light streaming in from the window.

'It's a lovely, smooth fit.' She ran her fingers around the band and then she jolted, suddenly realising something.

'Are you okay?' he said.

'Eh, yes...' she said hesitantly. 'I've just realised...this is the first time I've ever worn a wedding ring.'

She glanced up at Neil and there was a moment between them that she felt but couldn't quite explain.

He sensed it too.

'Well, I should be going,' she said, slipping the ring off and giving it back to him. In her haste her fingers brushed against his hand, and there was that frisson again.

Having had a look around, she wished she could stay longer to watch how he cut the gold and fashioned it into rings. But she needed to leave to gather her thoughts and the disarray of her feelings.

He saw her out.

'Thanks again for breakfast.' She tapped the book. 'I promise I'll look after this and give it back to you soon.'

'I hope it's of use to you. And I'd love to see the designs you make from it, if you're not too busy.'

She nodded. 'I'd be happy to show you.'

'Great.'

Smiling, she walked down the garden path and headed back to her cottage. She put the book safely on the hall table, and then headed out to the shops for fresh milk and groceries — and gossip. Hopefully she wouldn't be one of the topics.

CHAPTER THREE

'...And then Gaven posted her through her bedroom window—' Etta cut short her description of Penny's encounter with the laird.

Two other ladies were eager to hear the latest gossip, but stared guiltily when they saw Penny walk into the bakery.

The two–storey bakery was set in the heart of the main street and had a modern vintage ambiance. A fire burned in the hearth and old–fashioned glass lamps created a welcoming glow. Copper pans on the wall behind the counter gleamed under the lights, and ceramic vintage teapots sat on the shelf beside the array of tea blends sold. Penny loved the light cream decor and spotlights illuminating the glass counter and display cabinets filled with everything from patisserie specials like glazed fruit tarts to rhubarb and custard cake.

Penny had bought her groceries from the wee shop in the main street, but she enjoyed the bakery's oatmeal bread and intended buying a fresh loaf before heading back to her cottage. She hadn't expected to walk in to find the ladies gossiping about her in the bakery.

'I was telling Aileen and Sylvia about your adventure last night with the laird,' Etta explained. Etta was in her fifties, with silvery blonde hair, a neat appearance, and was a key member of the crafting bee. She was a keen knitter and ran her small knitting business from her home in one of the cottages near

Penny. She'd been the first to welcome Penny to the local community, arriving on her doorstep with a home baked cake.

Penny smiled tightly, but she didn't blame them for gossiping. It was part of the village community. No secrets, but plenty of well–meaning interest in what was going on, especially if it involved the laird.

Aileen and Sylvia, both in their early thirties, were bee members too, and all three of them were sitting at one of the tables near the front windows of the bakery chatting over a pot of tea and slices of Scottish fruit loaf and tea bread.

Aileen's dark brown hair was swept up at the sides with clasps emphasising her porcelain complexion and hazel eyes. She owned the quilt shop and sold bundles of fabric and thread as well as beautiful quilts.

Sylvia was a sweet maker and worked alongside her aunt in the local sweet shop. Vintage, traditional and all sorts of sweets were sold in the pretty little shop. Sylvia's shoulder–length blonde hair was a few shades lighter than Penny's and she bore a delicate beauty with lovely green eyes that seemed filled with curiosity.

Penny didn't know Aileen or Sylvia well and hoped to get to know them better at the bee nights.

Bradoch, the owner of the bakery, stood behind the counter pretending to be so busy arranging the raspberry doughnuts and buttery pastry treats on display that he hadn't overheard the gossip.

Bradoch wore chef whites and was in his mid thirties, handsome, with dark hair and dark blue eyes. He'd trained as a patisserie chef and had taken over the bakery from his grandfather, and added tables at the front to create a hub for tea, hot chocolate, cakes and chatter.

Penny loved the welcoming aroma of the bakery — fresh baked bread mingled with the delicious scent of chocolate, vanilla and cake baking. She hadn't had a proper conversation with Bradoch as he was always busy serving in the bakery, but she liked him. He was cheery.

Etta invited Penny to join them. 'Come and have a cuppa with us.'

Penny swithered, wondering whether to spare ten minutes for a quick cup of tea. 'I've a busy morning ahead.'

'Och! Come on and have a tea and a natter,' Etta encouraged her.

It didn't take much to encourage Penny, and she went over and sat down at the table.

'Can we have another cup please, Bradoch?' Etta called over to him.

Bradoch had already put a cup and a fresh pot of tea on a tray and came over to serve it up to Penny along with a slice of tea bread and a little pat of butter on the side of the plate. Bradoch made his own butter from double cream.

'I only came in to buy an oatmeal loaf,' said Penny.

'I'll put one aside for you,' Bradoch told her and went back to the counter and wrapped one up for her. They were popular and sold well, so she was glad he'd done this.

Penny nodded her thanks.

Aileen and Sylvia leaned forward, eager to hear what had happened with Penny and the laird.

Penny explained the details, culminating in Gaven helping her climb in her bedroom window.

'He said he posted you like a letter,' Etta remarked.

'Did he now?' Penny sounded slightly miffed. 'I suppose he's told everyone what a fool I was.'

Etta shook her head. 'No, he only confided in Jessy. She works for him at the castle. He told her what happened last night. Jessy phoned to tell me.'

Penny sighed. It wasn't entirely his fault that everyone would soon know the gossip.

'But that wasn't the only reason Jessy called,' said Etta. 'Gaven says the function room is available tonight and wondered if we'd like to have our bee night a wee bit earlier. He's making no charge for it. And serving us tea and cake.'

The ladies looked hopeful that Penny would come along.

'It's short notice, but...' Etta shrugged.

Penny pondered for a moment and then thought... 'Yes, okay. I'll bring my sewing. I can sew at the bee instead of sitting at home.'

'Great, I've put the word out to the other members, and so far they're all coming along tonight,' said Etta.

Penny spread the butter on her tea bread and took a bite. It tasted delicious.

'Jessy said that Gaven seemed quite intrigued by you,' Etta told Penny.

Penny took a sip of tea. 'Really? I can't think why.'

'Is it true you insulted him?' Aileen asked her.

'Yes, I didn't know he was the laird at first,' Penny admitted. 'I blurted out that I thought he was grumpy and standoffish.'

The ladies laughed.

'I doubt that endeared me to him,' said Penny, enjoying her buttered tea bread.

Etta shrugged. 'Well, according to Jessy, he was asking all sorts of questions about you.'

'What sort of questions?' Penny asked her.

'Were you single,' Etta told her.

Penny almost choked on her tea. 'He told me he'd read my website. He knew about my sewing and mending.'

'It sounds like the laird has a fancy for you,' Aileen suggested.

Penny held her hands up. 'I'm not eager to get romantically involved with anyone. I've enough to do getting my business up and running here.'

Sylvia nodded. 'I know what you mean. I've only been here since Christmas. I came to work in the sweet shop with my aunt. I worked for a bakery in Edinburgh and trained in confectionary making. But I always wanted to make sweeties, and I'm still settling in and I don't want to rush into any romances at the moment.'

Aileen agreed. 'There are quite a few eligible men, from farmers to men like the laird and...' she glanced over at Bradoch and then added, 'and Bradoch the handsome baker.' She nudged Sylvia.

'I'm not interested in dating Bradoch at the moment,' Sylvia said, keeping her voice down.

'Has he asked you out yet?' Etta said to her.

Sylvia shook her head. 'No, we talk about sweeties. He buys them for his cakes and as extras for his customers.'

Aileen wasn't convinced. 'There's a rumour that Bradoch is sweet on you, Sylvia.'

Sylvia blushed. 'Shhh! Keep your voice down. He'll hear us talking about him.'

They looked over and saw Bradoch writing a list on his notepad. He tore it out and then headed over to their table.

'He's coming over,' Sylvia hissed. 'Talk about something else.'

'So what type of thread do you use for your mending, Penny?' said Aileen.

'Embroidery floss is my go–to thread,' Penny told her.

Bradoch smiled as he approached their table. 'Sorry to interrupt, but could I order more jelly sweets and tablet from you?' He handed the list to Sylvia.

Sylvia skim–read the list and smiled up at him. 'Yes, I'll drop these off to you later.'

Bradoch smiled back at her. 'I'd appreciate it. I've been adding the sweets to some of my cakes and customers are enjoying them.' Taking a deep breath, he left them to finish their tea and went back to the counter to serve other customers coming in.

'He fancies you,' Aileen said to Sylvia.

Sylvia's cheeks were flushed. 'He's nice, and of course handsome, but romance complicates everything. I broke up with my boyfriend just before I came here. I want some time to myself before getting involved again.'

'That's exactly how I feel,' said Penny. 'I didn't have a break–up though. I've been so busy with my work.'

'What if Gaven asks you to have dinner with him?' Etta asked Penny.

'I'll tell him I'll be friends with him, like I am now with Neil.'

Etta blinked, and Sylvia and Aileen stared at Penny.

'You're friendly with the goldsmith?' Etta sounded surprised.

'He made me pancakes for breakfast,' Penny told them.

'The goldsmith made your breakfast?' Etta shouted.

Bradoch and the customers, mainly farmers in to collect their daily orders of fresh bread, rolls and tattie scones, looked over and stared at them.

'And I use gold metallic effect embroidery thread for all sorts of mending,' Penny said loud enough for the eavesdroppers to hear her.

Bradoch frowned, wondering if he'd misheard Etta's remark.

The ladies pretended to talk about sewing, and Bradoch and the customers continued with their business.

The women leaned forward and wanted to hear everything that had happened between Neil and Penny.

Drinking their tea, they listened while Penny told them everything.

Etta seemed particularly surprised. 'Neil is a fine looking man.'

'He's very tall and elegant,' Sylvia added.

'And classy,' said Aileen. 'Though he keeps himself to himself, so I don't really know him.'

'He's rich. I know that for sure,' Etta told them. 'He comes from money, and has made himself a small fortune from the jewellery he makes. Custom makes. Exclusive pieces for clients, including film stars.'

Sylvia didn't even know that snippet. 'Is that true?'

Etta nodded firmly. 'He was featured in one of the main newspapers. He made the engagement ring for a Hollywood star and wedding rings for those in the entertainment industry.'

'Etta showed me the feature,' Aileen confirmed. 'The goldsmith is very successful.'

Penny frowned. 'He seemed friendly enough to me. He's let me borrow photographs of flowers from his garden for my embroidery designs.'

Etta smiled. 'Maybe the goldsmith has a romantic interest in you, Penny.'

Penny brushed the suggestion aside, but couldn't help blushing. 'He was just being neighbourly.'

'Did you get to try on any of his expensive gold jewellery?' Sylvia asked Penny.

'Yes, a wedding ring. It's the first time I've ever worn one.'

'It won't be the last,' Etta told her knowingly.

Filled with tea, buttered tea bread, gossip and butterflies of excitement, Penny headed back to her cottage. She was looking forward to the crafting bee night at the castle, but felt a bit discombobulated thinking about Gaven and the things Etta had confided.

Was Gaven interested in her? Was she interested in him? And what about Neil?

She shook the thought from her mind, and breathed in the fresh morning air as she carried her groceries home.

A pale blue sunlit sky reflected off the surface of the loch, and the white cottages scattered around the area stood out against the heather and greenery. Breathing in the calm beauty of the Highlands, she unlocked the door and went inside her cottage to get on with her day.

She'd a lot of work to tackle before the bee night — lots of floral designs for a start.

Setting up her sketch paper, pencils, and fine tip, black ink pens, she sat down at the table near the back window of the living room that she'd made into her desk, and looked through the flower photographs Neil had given her. Pansies, she told herself firmly. She definitely needed those for her new floral spring designs. And snowdrops and crocus.

Steeped in her sketches, she started to focus on her artwork, but thoughts of Neil and having breakfast with him kept drifting through her mind.

But as the designs started to take shape on the paper, and were ready to be inked for the final artwork of the patterns, she became lost in her work, continuing through lunch with nothing more than a cup of tea, forging on to get as much done before it was time to attend the crafting bee.

The daylight had mellowed to a golden glow that filled the living room of her cottage. Easing the tension from her shoulders, she put her pen down and glanced out the back window.

Far up on the hillside, the twilight sky bore bands of pink and lilac mixed with the amber glow.

She checked the time. The bee night wasn't for another hour yet, so she put her boots and jacket on and decided to go for an invigorating walk up the hill to unwind after a full working day.

Walking up the hill recently had become something she loved to do, especially early in the morning or at twilight. There was something wonderful about feeling the soft heather and grass beneath her boots, the scent of the clear air and standing at the top of the hill gazing up at the sky and the surrounding countryside that stretched for miles around. She felt as if she was part of it all. It was like standing in a beautiful painting, enjoying the view.

Breathing it all in, she stood at the top of the hill for several minutes, and then as the sky started to deepen to brilliant blues, she headed back down. She saw her cottage lit up at the bottom of the hill. And there was Neil's cottage lit up too. He'd be in there making jewellery in his workshop.

She was still thinking about him as she got halfway down the hill and then noticed that the back door to his cottage was open and that she could see the tall, broad shouldered silhouette standing there. Was he looking at her? Or was he breathing in the early evening after working all day?

Walking on, careful not to tumble on the thick patches of heather, she saw him wave to her.

'Busy day?' he called to her as she got nearer.

'Yes, but productive. Those flower photos were very handy. I've drawn lots of sketches and inked several finished pieces.'

'I'm glad they were of use to you.'

'I'll let you see them soon — and give you the book back.'

He nodded and smiled. 'So are you working late again tonight?'

By now she was right outside his back garden fence. 'No, I'm going to the crafting bee at the castle. Gaven told the ladies that the function room is available this evening, so we're all getting together at seven.'

'Are you having dinner there?'

'No, I'm having a light dinner then getting ready to go to the castle. Apparently tea and cake are on offer.'

'A light dinner?'

Penny nodded.

He thumbed behind him. 'I've just taken a cheese soufflé out of the oven. Is that light enough? You're welcome to join me.'

'Oh, Neil, I can't keep eating your food...'

'I won't eat a whole soufflé. I couldn't make a small one, and it won't keep, so...' he gestured that she was welcome to come in.

She hesitated and then sighed. 'Okay, but you'll have to let me return the favour sometime and cook dinner for you.'

'You've twisted my arm,' he said smiling.

There wasn't a rear gate and so Penny thought she'd climb over the back fence instead of trailing round to the front of the cottage. The fence wasn't high.

Unfortunately, her jacket got snagged on a nail and as she tried to unhook it, she tumbled and ended up entangled in the hedging on the other side of the fence.

Neil rushed to her rescue, and despite her protests that she was fine, he lifted her up because it was the easiest and quickest way to get her over the fence and hedging.

He should've put her down immediately, but he paused, holding her in his strong arms under the twilight sky.

Penny had instinctively put her arm around Neil's shoulders and felt the lean muscles beneath his shirt. His sleeves were rolled up as if he'd been working, either in his workshop or cooking the soufflé. Either way, her hand brushed against his bare forearms causing a surge of electric energy to ignite within her.

And then he put her down gently.

She let him lead the way into the kitchen, feeling her heart beat strong and fast.

Inside the kitchen, the warmth from the oven wrapped itself around her. The tasty aroma of the cheddar cheese he'd used in his recipe sparked her appetite, and the bright but cosy lighting created a welcoming and homely feeling.

Penny shrugged her jacket off, hung it over the back of a chair, and washed her hands at the sink, as if slotting into the rhythm of Neil's home life was a custom fit.

His kitchen was cosy, and she liked the traditional light wooden dresser, table, chairs and cupboards. His dinner set was top–quality white porcelain embellished with a traditional floral design. But on the dresser shelves was an eclectic mix of other patterns on the porcelain side plates, bowls, cups, mugs and two ceramic teapots. Beautiful little bees and butterflies were part of the designs, and colourful bunting that created a vintage feel.

'I'll serve up the soufflé if you make the tea,' he said, selecting two matching dinner plates from the dresser.

'Deal,' Penny told him, picking two floral and bee mugs, and wondering if anyone had seen Neil lifting her up and carrying her into his cottage. If so, that would be more gossip for the ladies to chatter about.

CHAPTER FOUR

Neil served up the cheese soufflé with salad and cherry tomatoes, and they sat down at the kitchen table to enjoy their dinner.

Penny tasted the soufflé and nodded. It was light and airy with a delicious cheese flavour. 'If you ever decide on a second career, you'd nail it as a chef. This is one of the tastiest soufflés I've had.'

Neil smiled at the compliment.

'Really, I'm well–travelled, and this is excellent. I love the taste of the Scottish cheddar.'

'Well–travelled?' He sounded interested.

'Hmmm,' she murmured, enjoying another mouthful of the soufflé. 'You name it, I've probably been there.'

'So you enjoy travelling?'

'Nooo, I'm a homebody by nature, but my parents travelled extensively since I was born. My father was a businessman and his work took him all over the globe. We were rarely in the same place twice, or for any length of time.'

'Where are you from originally?'

'I was born in Scotland, in Fife.'

'Ah, the Kingdom of Fife. A beautiful part of Scotland.'

'It is. I barely remember it. We left to live in France when I was three, then on to Canada, America, back to the UK, London mainly, then off to Europe and Australia, sometimes popping back to Scotland to visit my grandparents in Fife.'

'Quite the whirlwind upbringing.'

'It was. My parents thrive on it. They're still travelling. They're somewhere in Europe at the moment.' She sighed. 'They're happy, and I do love my parents, I just don't love being unsettled. We didn't even have many belongings on our travels. Important items were kept with my grandparents, like a base, while we circled the globe.' She paused and looked thoughtful. 'I think that's why I got into sewing and mending.'

Neil ate his dinner and was interested in what she was saying.

'The only things that went with me were my clothes and a few precious toys, but often the toys were left behind and they'd buy me new ones. But I hung on to items of clothing — dresses and jackets, jeans and cosy cardigans, things that had texture and comfort. They were like an anchor to everything, while the world whizzed by in an ever–changing location.' She shrugged. 'Of course, I'd grow out of some things, but I learned to sew, and I taught myself to mend worn items so that they'd last longer before I had to discard them.'

Neil's eyes took on a heartfelt look as he gazed at her across the table. Those gorgeous, pale aqua eyes showed he understood and cared about everything she was telling him. He felt sad for the little girl who mended her clothes so she could make them last when nothing else did.

'I became quite the expert at taking down the hems of my jeans and skirts as I grew a bit taller. My parents were happy to buy me thread for sewing and encouraged my artistic tendencies. I loved to embroider strawberries and cherries on my clothes. If there was somewhere to stitch one of those, I'd embroider it with flair. And flowers. All sorts of flowers from roses to bluebells and cornflowers.'

'How did you end up here?'

'One day, when I was all grown up, my parents made a pit stop home to Fife. When they left to continue touring the world, I stayed. I decided to jump off the carousel of countries and make a life in Fife. But I couldn't settle there. It didn't feel like home, because it wasn't really. I then moved to work for a fashion company in Glasgow, living in a flat in the city, and that didn't feel like home either. Then I was made redundant. But I'd been reading about people making a life for themselves in the Scottish Highlands. It sounded marvellous. And one day I saw the cottage advertised and I realised that it looked like the little cottage I'd embroidered years ago. I'd framed it. A white cottage with pretty curtains on the windows set in the Highlands. It was the strangest feeling, as if I'd stitched what I'd been hoping for, somewhere to call home.' She took a deep breath. 'So I made a big, bold move as they say to make a fresh start here. And now I'm sitting having dinner with you.' She smiled as if concluding her story. 'Your turn. What's your history, Neil? I confess that Etta and the ladies have told me a few snippets of gossip.'

'Gossip about me?' He sounded surprised. Then he realised. 'Ah, the money thing.'

Penny ate her dinner and nodded.

'Yes, it's true, I come from money, as they say. As for a second career...I did train as a chef alongside my father. My parents own a restaurant in Edinburgh. They thought I'd follow them into the family business. My grandmother helped out at the restaurant. But when I was a boy and they were busy with the restaurant, which was basically all the time, my grandfather used to look after me. He was a watchmaker and I loved to go to his shop and see him work. He'd work there until late at night, and we'd have dinner in his shop, and I'd watch him create these intricate pieces, but that's not what fascinated me the most. It was the gold of the watches. Something about it drew me to the gold. And I ventured into goldwork. I opened a workshop in Edinburgh, then moved to Glasgow to open a shop. That thrived for a few years, but then I realised I didn't need to be based there. I could set up my workshop anywhere. I came here for a holiday, to live in one of the castle's cabins, for an artisan break. I felt at home here. So when it came time to leave, I decided to stay, and bought this cottage. It was available, and I've set up my workshop here. My clients are mainly online, as they mostly were before.'

'I've heard you make jewellery for film stars.'

'I do. I've made pieces for the Hollywood actor, Bradley Goldsilver, and others such as Tiara Timberlane and Shaw Starlight.' He shrugged off the stardom aspect. 'But many of my customers are people looking for a custom made piece, especially rings, and I love designing and making those.' He glanced around him. 'While living here in a cottage in the

Highlands. Items are posted off by courier. It's the perfect scenario. Like you, this feels like home.'

Penny lifted up her mug of tea. 'Let's drink a toast. To our homes in the Scottish Highlands.'

Neil tipped his mug against hers and they drank a toast.

He smiled over at her. 'I didn't expect to become friends with someone like you, Penny. That's an added bonus.'

She blushed. 'I didn't expect to meet a goldsmith in the wilds. But you're one of those rare breeds I suppose.'

'We both are. Maybe that's why we get along so easily.'

'I'll drink to that,' she said.

They raised their cups and tipped them together again, and continued enjoying their dinner and conversation.

'What about someone special in your life?' she ventured to ask him.

'You mean romance?'

She nodded.

He shook his head. 'That's one area of my life where I've had little success. But I live in hope. I would like to find someone special, marry her and settle down.'

'At least you won't have to save up for an engagement ring.' The comment was out before she could edit it. 'I don't mean to sound trite,' she apologised instantly.

Neil wasn't offended. 'It's true. I'll design and make the engagement ring and wedding rings myself. I'll charge myself a small fortune,' he joked.

Penny laughed.

'Then I'd make her an eternity ring,' he added. 'And anniversary rings as the years go by.'

'Rings? As in more than one?'

'Oh yes. Gold with diamonds, sapphires, semi–precious gems.'

'A lucky lady.'

'I'd spoil her rotten, if she'd let me.' Those pale blue eyes of his looked right at her.

'I'm sure she would. Whoever you marry, I'm certain you'll make the right choice.'

He nodded and smiled, then looked deep into his cup. 'What time is your bee night at the castle?'

'Oops! Seven o'clock. It's almost quarter to. I'll have to scarper and get ready.' She stood up. 'Thanks for dinner, Neil. Sorry I have to dash.'

He smiled warmly. 'Enjoy your evening.'

'I'll make dinner for you soon,' she promised, running out the front door to avoid having to climb the back fence again.

Neil stood lit up in the front doorway watching her hurry away to her cottage, giving him a cheery wave before she disappeared inside.

He breathed in the night air and gazed up at the starry sky — and felt an unexpected pang of envy. Gaven would no doubt be ready to welcome Penny to the castle. The impromptu crafting bee night was too convenient. He wondered if Gaven had arranged it sooner so he could see Penny again.

Neil took another deep breath of the brisk night air, then went inside, taking his suspicions with him and closing the door.

From experience, Penny knew she'd be asked about her mending methods, especially the visible mending, and the easiest way to explain about satin stitching patches on to jackets, mending torn seams on jeans, using appliqué and seed stitches to repair frayed cuffs and collars, and embellishing vintages pieces with embroidery motifs to breathe new life into them was to wear them to the bee night.

Her grey jeans were a prime example of how to jazz up rips on the legs with colourful patches stitched with embroidery thread. The thread was stitched across the tear and then another colour was woven through the straight stitches. She'd used two strands of variegated cobalt blue embroidery thread along with two strands of a hot pink colour. The thread patch looked great with the grey jeans. She's also sewn hexies on to the worn pockets made from ditsy print floral cotton fabric. Hexies were great for making quilts, something she'd done in the past, but they were a handy, pretty and sturdy way to make a patchwork repair to an area of clothing, especially jeans, T–shirts and tops. Her fabric stash was usually brimming with lots of spare pieces of fabric that she used for her patchwork and appliqué repair work. Recently, it had become slightly depleted and she planned to restock it soon.

She looked through the clothes hanging in her wardrobe and selected a pale blue cotton shirt. The collar and cuffs had become worn and she'd mended them with lots of tiny seed stitches, sewn with various colours of embroidery thread. The effect was one of her favourites and fun to stitch. The seed stitches created a scatter of colour and covered the worn areas. This was an easy way to extend the wear of a much–loved but well–worn shirt. The edges of the cuffs were so worn that she'd sewn fabric from her stash along the edges, giving a splash of fashionable colour and interest to the plain shirt.

Over the shirt she put on a white cardigan she'd darned with crewel wool to mend the holes on the sleeves with Scotch darning. For this type of mending she used a wooden darning mushroom and stitched contrasting colours of crewel wool across the worn elbows to repair them. And she'd darned the small holes in the front of the cardigan with crewel wool to create circles of primary colours. The plain white cardigan was now an artistically enhanced piece in her wardrobe, as were others like it. Mending wasn't just for fabric clothing, it was for knitted garments too. To emphasise the new look of it, she'd replaced the original white buttons with blue, pink, yellow and red buttons to add more pops of colour to the cardigan's redesigned look.

She owned several cotton and canvas bags that she'd made from plain fabric and prints, then covered with patches, embroidery and appliqué. She used the bags for shopping and as craft bags. She filled the bag that had a beach hut and bunting appliqué design with a T–shirt she was currently mending, along with a handmade needle book that had needles and embroidery thread in it, so she could work on mending the T–shirt during the bee evening.

Before putting on her boots, she shrugged on her denim jacket in the hall. The jacket was a great example of her mending methods using embroidery motifs and patches sewn on to it.

She'd brushed her hair smooth and refreshed her makeup, and was ready to go to the castle.

Taking a deep breath, she headed out into the night.

Gaven striped off his comfy, check flannel shirt and cargo trousers as the hands on the old–fashioned clock on his bedside table warned him that it was nearing seven.

Wearing his favourite casuals in shades of brown wouldn't cut it tonight. He needed to up his game if he wanted to impress Penny.

As he threw on a clean, dark blue shirt over his lean muscled torso, he glanced out the window of his turret bedroom. The turret peeked over the tip of the hill, giving him a view of the loch, cottages, including Penny's cottage, and the distant twinkling lights of the main street. It had a luxurious double bed with deep blue silk sheets and a matching satin bedspread.

The antique furnishings were highly polished, and a large landscape painting, depicting the loch and a stormy sky, worth a small fortune, was on one of the walls.

This had been his room since he was a boy, and although he could've moved down a floor to one of the larger bedrooms, he preferred being tucked away in the turret with a view of the loch and surrounding village. Besides, he liked the seclusion of it. No, correct that. The privacy. He wasn't a recluse despite the standoffish accusations he'd had over the years, including last night from Penny. He was a busy man with a castle to run and financial dealings in the city that kept him on a whirlwind schedule that barely left time for anything except work. Socialising was on the back burner this year again, though he was prepared to make time for Penny, if she happened to actually like him. Which he doubted. He wished he could retract his comments to Jessy. Now the gossip was bound to have reached Penny's ears. She'd accuse him of talking about her behind her back. Which he had, but that was beside the point.

Buttoning his shirt as quickly as his fingers could fiddle with them, he jumped into a pair of dark, smart trousers, part of a suit hanging in his wardrobe, and then topped the look off with the silk backed waistcoat. The midnight blue silk matched his shirt. He was nothing if not coordinated, even if his feeling were scattered to the wind.

This was ridiculous, he told himself. He never got himself into such a tizzy over a girl. But there was something about Penny. He hadn't been able to stop thinking about lifting her up, feeling her feminine softness trust him to help her out of her predicament. In her place, he wouldn't have trusted a complete stranger, a man running along the loch late at night, dressed in stealthy black gear as if he was on a midnight raid. Penny had a trusting heart. He liked that. He liked Penny.

Calm down, he told himself. She might not even turn up to the bee night. He'd twisted himself into a knot trying to orchestrate it almost a week earlier than scheduled. He'd furtively bumped a couple of the guests dinner plans in the function room, offering them a free dinner in the castle's bar restaurant instead. They'd been happy to dine there, especially as he'd thrown gratis whisky into the mix. But Jessy knew what he'd been up to. She didn't say anything, but she knew, and would no doubt pass along her suspicions to Etta and others.

He let out a huge sigh. What a pickle he'd got himself into.

The hands on the clock moved closer to seven.

With minutes to spare, he dashed downstairs and then walked the last set of stairs casually. The main staircase led to the hotel style reception area where he planned to make a sauntering entrance.

But instead of the efficient milling around of staff getting ready to welcome the crafting bee members and attend to other guests in the castle popping down for dinner, there was the rumblings of chaos.

Just what he needed, he thought sarcastically, and then set about trying to tame the trouble.

Penny walked the short distance to the castle, using the turrets as a compass. It wasn't far and the evening light reflected off the surface of the loch creating a glow across the landscape.

A well–worn path across the grass steepled upwards towards the castle grounds. Ornate fencing and a large, open metal gate with overarching bows created an impressive entrance. The castle itself was equally impressive, and the front entrance was all lit up and the double doors open in welcoming. The windows on the ground floor where she presumed the function room was situated were aglow, along with other windows on the two floors above it. The two turrets were in darkness and she wondered if anyone lived in them or whether they were more for show than practicality.

A gravel path led the way to the entrance, and she felt her boots crunch on it as she viewed the extensive surrounding gardens that blended with the landscape. How far did the castle's estate stretch, she wondered. Far enough to include the log cabins, a couple of cottages and what looked like two chalets near the cabins. The perfect location of artisan holidays, she thought, picturing that she'd have enjoyed a crafty break there herself. Lights shone from the cabins that looked like expensive retreats. Nothing rough and ready about these hideaways. They looked fairly new, certainly not built in the time of the castle. They were like modern holiday homes and would no doubt have all the mod cons.

It seemed that a forest bordered the castle on the side of the cabins and chalets, so she couldn't tell what was beyond it. Probably more trees and the river she'd heard about. Or the cove. She'd need to have a look at a local map and get her bearings, learn the lay of the land.

Sounds of chatter and the aroma of dinners wafted out of the front entrance as Penny approached. A suddenly surge of excitement fluttered through her, and she took a steadying breath, looking forward to the bee night.

But then the chatter sounded clearer and she realised...

Pandemonium rather than pleasantries was playing out in the castle's reception. Something was wrong. Whatever could it be?

CHAPTER FIVE

Gaven stood at the reception desk fielding suggestions from Jessy, Etta, Aileen and several other people — staff and members of the crafting bee.

The scattered conversation indicated that a guest, an author staying in one of the castle's cabins on a writer's break to finish the last two chapters of his latest, and much anticipated, thriller novel, had lost something of importance. Apparently, the author was there because he'd lost his muse and hoped the quiet surroundings would help him finish writing the concluding chapters to meet the book's impending deadline. However, earlier in the evening the author had been distracted by another guest, a very attractive one, and she'd caused him to misplace the lucky charm he wore on a gold chain necklace — a small gold pen.

'It couldn't have bounced far from the bed,' Aileen reasoned. 'Shine a torch on the carpet.'

'What was she doing in his cabin anyway?' said Etta.

'They were having fun, enjoying an evening of artistic togetherness,' Jessy told her. Jessy was in her fifties, and wore her brown hair in a chignon. She'd worked at the castle for years.

Gaven sighed heavily. 'Have the staff searched the cabin thoroughly?'

Jessy nodded. 'They've looked everywhere. He's very upset. He says he's lost his muse and now the last thing he needs is to lose his lucky charm.'

Penny buttoned her lips, and peered into the function room. The other ladies were setting up their sewing, quilting, knitting and other crafts for the evening. They were buzzing with excitement, and she wondered whether she should join them and sidestep the furore.

A moment later, one of Gaven's key staff, Walter, a sturdy man in his fifties, came running in, holding his fist aloft. 'The panic's over. I found it.' He opened his hand to reveal the shiny gold pen safely in his palm.

'Where was it?' asked Jessy. 'We even searched the bedding.'

Walter lowered his voice. 'I had a private chat with the author. He said that their playful antics got a bit out of hand. In the heat of the moment the lady grabbed his pen and it shot off across the bedroom. I worked out that the trajectory would've sent it flying near the window. I had a look, and there it was.'

Gaven acknowledged Walter's initiative. 'Well done.'

'But the wee link to attach it to the chain is broken. It's all bendy. I thought I'd try to straighten it with a pair of pliers.' Walter went to head off to get his tool box.

'No,' Gaven insisted. 'It's obviously precious to our guest. Take it to the goldsmith. See if he can repair it properly and have it ready for collection in the morning.'

Walter nodded, grabbed an envelope from the reception desk, put the broken chain and charm in it, and hurried away.

A sigh of relief rippled through reception, and it was then that Gaven noticed Penny had arrived.

'Good–evening, Penny,' Gaven said, smiling at her. 'It's not usually so chaotic here. But everything's okay now.' He swept his hand towards the function room. 'Let me show you through. Most of the ladies have arrived.'

No more was said about the pandemonium, and the offer of tea and cake replaced the drama.

'Gaven's looking very smart this evening,' Aileen whispered to Etta as they headed into the function room.

Etta nodded and glanced in Penny's direction. 'I think he's trying to impress someone.'

They exchanged a knowing nod and then settled themselves at one of the tables.

Sylvia was already seated and casting on stitches to knit a scarf using lovely double knit yarn.

Penny admired the traditional decor of the room — cream walls with oak beams, and a polished wooden floor that doubled as a dance floor for party nights. Floor to ceiling glass patio doors were draped with burgundy velvet curtains, and two chandeliers hung from the high ceiling. Sconces lit the walls, and a log fire burned in the large fireplace at the far end of the room. She could feel the warmth of it from where she was seated at Etta, Aileen and Sylvia's table.

Introductions were made, allowing Penny to meet the other ladies, and then staff began to bring silver trolleys filled with cakes and tea through and set up a mini feast on a buffet table where members could help themselves.

'Gaven's lingering,' Sylvia whispered to Etta.

Etta agreed. Usually Gaven made himself scarce on bee nights. But here he was, smiling, admiring one of the quilts that Aileen unfolded from her craft bag.

'A lovely quilt you're making, Aileen,' said Gaven. He sounded as if he knew what he was talking about, when the opposite was true. He didn't know half the things the members made. Words and phrases like hexies, English paper piecing, whitework and crewelwork were like a whole different language to him.

'Thank you, Gaven,' said Aileen, getting ready to hand stitch the binding on to her quilt.

Gaven then went over to the buffet table to ensure the staff were setting it up with the extra cake he'd ordered. Any excuse to linger nearby.

One of the other ladies, working on her crochet, a lovely shawl, commented to Etta. 'Gaven's up to something.'

'He's looking very handsome this evening,' Etta remarked.

Sylvia nodded. 'He suits that waistcoat. It shows off his broad shoulders and lean waist.'

The other ladies sitting around the table agreed.

Etta nudged Penny. 'We suspect he's titivated himself up for your benefit.'

Penny pretended she was busy taking her needle book and sewing from her craft bag. 'I hadn't noticed.'

'He's always tidy,' Aileen admitted, 'but he's more casual when it's our bee nights. You'd think he'd been away on business and didn't have time to change.'

'Shhh! Here he comes,' Sylvia whispered.

'Help yourself to the tea and cake, ladies,' Gaven told them.

'You're really spoiling us this evening,' Etta remarked. The generous selection of cakes included chocolate layer cake, Victoria sponge filled with strawberries and cream, and rich fruit cake with a crown of almonds, red and green glacé cherries, and other crystallised fruit like decorative jewels.

Gaven brushed this suggestion aside. 'Think of it as a welcome back to your bee nights at the castle.'

'It's good to be back,' said Etta.

The other ladies nodded in agreement, as the sound of sewing machines started to whir in the background.

Quilters sat alongside dressmakers, talking about fabric.

Robin, a textile artist and knitwear model, had brought along a piece of fabric artwork she'd been hand stitching with embroidery thread. She'd painted an atmospheric sky on to white cotton fabric, and added pieces of blue, green and amber chiffon and lace to create a textured seascape. Robin was very attractive with long strawberry blonde hair and a porcelain complexion. She'd used the money she made from being a knitwear model to help establish herself as a textile artist, working from one of the local cottages.

Robin also liked to quilt, and particularly enjoyed making small quilted items like mug rugs, oven mitts, pincushions, along with aprons and sewing machine covers.

The crafts the ladies were working on included embroidery, knitting, quilting, dressmaking, crochet, papercraft, scrapbooking and rag doll making. The skills were shared happily.

Three sewing machines were set on tables at the side of the function room for the members to use. The machines were kept in the function room cupboard and Gaven's staff had put them on the tables. The previous summer, the bee members had intended clubbing together to buy the machines from the bee's small fund. But Gaven insisted on paying for the sewing machines, allowing them to keep their funds for other things. Contributing to the local community's activities was something he took on as their laird.

Gaven smiled at Penny. 'I hope you'll allow me to give you a tour of the castle during the evening.'

Several sets of eyebrows raised, but not a comment from any of the ladies.

'Eh, yes, that would be lovely,' Penny told him.

'I'll let you get on with your crafting, ladies.' Gaven smiled and then strode away.

'A tour of the castle,' Etta said to Penny. 'He's definitely pulling out all the stops this evening.'

'He's never offered me a tour,' one of the ladies complained jokingly.

Penny tried to contain the blush that was forming across her cheeks.

'I just want to see what you're all making,' Penny told them. This was true.

'Maybe Gaven will take you upstairs to his private quarters and show you his turret,' Etta said, causing the ladies to giggle.

Penny smiled. 'You're incorrigible, Etta.'

'I always have been,' Etta admitted, and then she showed Penny the jumper she was knitting. A beautiful Fair Isle, man's jumper.

'I can knit,' said Penny. 'But basic things. Nothing as complicated as your jumper.'

'I'd be happy to show you how to knit a pattern like this,' said Etta. 'We all exchange techniques, crafting skills, share fabric and yarn from our stashes.'

'I'd love to see how you do your creative mending,' Sylvia said to Penny.

The other ladies were keen too.

'I wore these items to show you the visible mending I use for clothes,' Penny told them. She took her jacket off and it was passed around for them to inspect.

'Is this embroidery thread you've used for these patches?' one of the ladies asked.

'Yes, stranded cotton, usually two strands,' Penny told them. 'I used one or two strands to embroider the flower motifs, satin stitching the petals and split stitching the stems.' She pointed to the bluebells she'd embroidered on the jacket.

'I love the idea of visible mending,' said Etta. 'The lovely colours of the embroidery thread creates beautiful designs.'

'That's what I love about it,' Penny agreed. She showed them the crewelwork stitching on her cardigan. 'I used crewel wool to embroider and mend my cardigan.'

'I think I'll give it a go,' said Etta.

'Most of the members could do this type of creative mending,' Penny told them. 'But almost anyone, even with basic sewing skills, could try their hand at mending their clothes. All you need is a needle and thread. Start with a few stitches using embroidery thread, or ordinary sewing thread, and mend a hole or rip in an item of clothing. Don't hide the repair, make a feature of it.'

'I have a few items that could do with repairing so I can get the use out of them again,' one of the ladies said.

'Socks are what I need to mend. I've several pairs of socks I knitted but there are holes in the heels. I've washed them, but I don't wear them because of the holes. I love those socks so I haven't thrown them out. I know the work I put in knitting them,' said Sylvia.

'I always darn the holes in my socks.' Penny slipped her boot off and gave Sylvia a peek at the sock she was wearing that she'd darned.

'I'm definitely going to repair all my abandoned socks,' said Sylvia.

'I'd like to try mending shirts and tops that are showing signs of wear and tear,' one of the ladies said to Penny.

'Start with a few easy, straight stitches, running stitches and seed stitches on something like an old tea towel for practise,' said Penny. 'Or an old pillowcase. Anything where you can try out the mending stitches without fussing about getting them right first time.'

'Tea towels!' exclaimed Etta. 'Now that's something I'll have a go at mending.'

'I find mending is fun,' Penny told them. 'It's relaxing, and I enjoy making something fit for use again, and working with lovely coloured embroidery thread. I like crewel wool too, and pieces of fabric, especially for needleturn appliqué. Ribbon trims are so pretty too. I love making the repairs into new designs.'

'I have a lot of items hanging in my wardrobe that I don't wear anymore because they're a bit worn,' one of the ladies said to Penny. 'But now I'm thinking about mending them too.'

'I bought a bargain bundle of vintage dresses and skirts online,' another member explained. 'I washed the clothes and hung them up on my to–do rail with the intention of repairing any rips or holes using invisible mending.' She sighed. 'I think that's why they're still hanging there. Invisible mending takes a bit of skill and I'm not so confident with that. But seeing your visible mending techniques has got me thinking about making a start on repairing them.'

'I like the patterns you create with your bold colours of thread and patches,' a member hand stitching a quilt commented to Penny. 'I have worn collars on shirts and blouses I'd like to mend but I'm not sure about using such bright colours to draw attention to the mending. And yet I do like your ideas.'

Penny showed them the collar of her light blue shirt. 'I've added loads of seeds stitches to my collar with embroidery thread in colours that stand out, but you could use thread that matches the colour of your shirts. The stitches will strengthen and repair the wear on the collar but blend in nicely.'

The woman nodded. 'I'll try that.'

Aileen eyed Penny's craft bag that was hanging on the back of the chair. 'The beach hut appliqué on your bag is gorgeous. Did you make the pattern yourself?'

'I design all my own patterns for appliqué and embroidery,' Penny explained.

The crafting chatter continued until they stopped to enjoy their tea and cake.

Penny opted for a slice of the fruit cake topped with the almonds and glacé cherries.

Walter hurried up the path to Neil's cottage and knocked on the door.

Neil opened it and was surprised to see Walter standing there handing him the envelope containing the broken necklace. He was on nodding terms with Walter and knew he worked at the castle.

'Sorry to disturb you, Neil, but Gaven needs your help to mend a gold necklace belonging to one of his guests.' Walter explained the predicament.

'Leave it with me, Walter. I'll repair the damage.'

'Thank you. Send the repair bill to the castle.' Walter waved and hurried away.

'Is the bee night still going strong?' Neil called after him.

Walter paused. 'Yes, the ladies hadn't even had their tea and cake when I left.'

Neil smiled and nodded, and Walter hurried on.

Neil took the envelope inside and through to his workshop. He flicked on one of the lamps on his desk. A repair like this was easy, especially with his expert tools on hand, gold findings to attach the charm securely to the chain, and the impetus of knowing that the bee night was still on.

Gaven circled the function room waiting for the opportunity to invite Penny on a tour of the castle. But every time he saw her, she was busy sewing and talking to the ladies about their crafting. He didn't feel he could interrupt without disturbing her night.

Maybe he'd catch her at the end of the evening for a quick tour.

'I've always wanted to be part of a sewing or crafting bee,' Penny told the ladies.

'We have party nights for special occasions,' Etta told her. 'The castle is ideal as Gaven lets us have the use of the function room for buttons.'

The ladies were still crafting and chatting as Neil walked in. He wore an expensive silk tie with his shirt and looked tall and handsome. Seeing Penny sitting at one of the tables, he walked over, smiling.

'Neil!' Penny exclaimed. 'What are you doing here?' She was happy to see him, but wondered if there was something wrong.

He held up the envelope with the repaired necklace. 'I'm looking for Gaven or Walter. I've mended the broken chain.'

Jessy had been talking to Penny and the others, exchanging sewing tips. 'Gaven's probably in his room or his office behind reception. I'll let him know you're here.'

'Thanks,' said Neil.

'Come and sit with us,' Etta encouraged him.

Neil pulled up a chair and joined them.

Penny's heart beat increased seeing Neil sitting there looking particularly handsome.

'We've been having tea and cake,' Etta told him. 'Do you want a cuppa?'

'I wouldn't say no,' Neil replied.

One of the staff at the buffet table poured a cup of tea for Neil and gave him a slice of the Victoria cream sponge.

'I'll just sit here,' Neil said, sitting in his chair sipping his tea. 'Don't let me interrupt your crafting.'

'We were just telling Penny about the party nights we have here,' Etta explained to Neil.

'I heard the Christmas Eve ceilidh was wild,' he said.

'You should've joined us,' Aileen told him.

'I'll join in next time there's a party,' Neil promised, and then took a bite of his cake.

'We'll hold you to that, Neil,' Etta told him. 'We all heard you promise.'

He took a sip of his tea. 'No getting out of it now,' he joked. 'Not that I want to.'

'You've been a bit elusive,' Sylvia told him.

'You're right, but I intend to remedy that,' he said.

Jessy came hurrying over to their table. 'Gaven's in his room, but he's coming down.'

Neil ate his cake and nodded.

'You were quick to repair the gold chain,' Penny remarked to him.

'It was an easy repair, and as it's important to the author, I thought I'd pop up with it,' Neil explained.

Etta picked up her knitting and worked the Fair Isle pattern.

Neil looked interested. 'That's a great jumper.'

Etta held it up. 'It's a man's Fair Isle I'm making.'

Neil leaned closer and peered at it. 'I'm wondering if it has my name on it.'

Etta smiled. 'It's yours if you want it. I'm sure it would fit you. I was going to advertise it for sale on my website.'

'Don't. I'll buy it,' he said. 'It's something I'm in need of — nice, new, traditional style jumpers. And a couple of cardigans. I know we're coming into the spring, but I expect the evenings to still be brisk.'

Etta was delighted. 'I have other jumpers and a cardigan on my website. Have a look and let me know if you like anything, or I can knit to order in the colours you prefer.' Then Etta remembered that one of the other bee members, Sylvia's Aunt Muira, had been knitting a gorgeous man's cardigan in shades of classy neutrals.

'Muira,' Etta called over to her. 'Come and let Neil see that lovely cardigan you're knitting.'

Muira brought her cardigan over and Neil liked it immediately.

Penny was enjoying watching Neil's genuine warmth as he selected items from them.

'This has been very handy,' Neil remarked. 'Tea, cake, and a new wardrobe of clothes. If anyone has a set of oven mitts, that would be ideal.'

Robin offered him a pair of quilted mitts. She'd brought them along to show the members her latest patchwork designs.

'Perfect,' said Neil, insisting on paying full price for everything.

The light–hearted banter exchanged was interrupted when Gaven came striding into the function room and walked up to their table. He looked at Neil.

'Walter would've picked up the necklace in the morning,' Gaven began. 'But thank you for sorting it so quickly.' He glanced around, seeing Neil sitting beside Penny and the other ladies, in the heart of the bee. 'I didn't know you were into crafting,' Gaven said to Neil.

'I'm into buying crafting items,' Neil shot back at him, sensing a flicker of rivalry between them. Nothing that would cause trouble, just enough to rankle each other.

'The ladies have kitted him out with jumpers, cardigans and oven mitts,' Penny said to Gaven.

'Excellent,' Gaven forced himself to say, trying to smile.

Walter came scurrying in. 'That was fast work,' he said to Neil, smiling happily. 'Will I hand the necklace in to the author's cabin?' he asked Gaven.

'I'll give it to him personally,' said Gaven.

Walter nodded and hurried away.

Neil handed the envelope to Gaven.

Gaven opened it and pulled out the necklace. The gold shone under the light of the chandeliers. 'Very nice.'

'I gave it a quick buff to bring up the lustre,' Neil explained.

Gaven put it carefully back into the envelope.

'Bill me for the full amount,' Gaven said to Neil.

Neil brushed the cost aside. 'It was an easy fix, and I've indulged in tea and cake here with the ladies. We'll call it even.'

'Fair enough,' said Gaven.

Walter came hurrying back and called into the function room. 'It's started raining, ladies. There was a flash of lightning over the hills in the distance. I think a storm is brewing.'

Penny sensed the tension between Gaven and Neil, and totally agreed.

Gaven hurried away to the author's cabin.

The ladies started to pack up their craft bags and head home before the full force of the storm arrived.

Neil stood up. 'My car is parked outside. Anyone want a lift home?' He glanced at Penny.

'Yes, thank you, Neil,' Penny said, not wanting to get soaked on the walk back to her cottage. It would be silly not to accept a lift from Neil as their cottages were near each other.

'Room for three more,' Neil announced, and found three eager ladies to take him up on his offer.

Aileen and Sylvia had driven up, and they offered lifts to Etta and others.

As the ladies arranged to help each other from getting soaked, even on the short trips home, Neil led Penny and the others out to his expensive, dark gold coloured car. He had the oven mitts with him, but the jumpers and cardigans he'd purchased had still to be finished or blocked properly before he received them.

By the time they were seated in Neil's car, Gaven was striding back from the author's cabin towards the castle.

Neil gave Gaven a cheery wave as he drove off with Penny in the passenger seat and three other ladies in the back.

'Gaven doesn't look happy,' one of the ladies remarked.

'I can't think why,' Neil said, glancing and smiling at Penny.

Penny couldn't help but smile back at Neil, and he drove on to the far side of the loch where the three women's cottages were situated. It made sense to drop them off and then drive Penny home.

Penny and Neil waved to the ladies, and then drove on, heading to their own side of the loch.

The sky was a thunderous arch of fast–moving, dark storm clouds.

'I love stormy nights like this.' Neil sounded excited.

'So do I,' Penny agreed.

'Are you in an adventurous mood?' he asked her.

Penny smiled. 'Maybe.'

'Want to watch the storm from one of the vantage points up on the hillside over there?' He motioned towards the hills that backed on to their cottages.

A surge of excitement charged through Penny. 'Okay, I'm up for it.' And then she leaned back in her seat as Neil drove them into the stormy night.

CHAPTER SIX

Neil parked his car in a viewing area near the top of the hills. The Highland landscape was a patchwork of fields and rolling hills with the stormy sky all around them.

'What a view,' said Penny.

'You should see it on calm nights when the stars are out, or on a clear morning. I like to walk up here a few times during the week,' Neil told her. 'It keeps me fit.'

'I haven't ventured this far, but I need to study a map or go exploring around the area. The snow and colder weather and being busy has kept me close to home.'

Neil reached over to the glove compartment. 'There's a map in here.' He lifted it out and opened it to show her the local area.

Penny leaned close, interested in seeing the lay of the land. 'I don't have a great sense of direction. Where are our cottages?'

'Over there, beside the loch,' he pointed to the location. 'This viewing area is here, not far from them.'

'Is that Gaven's castle?'

'Yes, and his estate covers quite a bit of land with the forest edging this area of the estate.' Neil indicated where it was on the map. 'The loch is located in the heart of everything nearby. The coast, with the cove is there.'

'It's not far,' Penny observed.

'No, but with all the hills and trees it's easy to think that we're far from the sea, when it's really only a ten to fifteen minutes drive away. I can recommend the bakery at the cove. They sell the most delicious lunches and ice cream. Though it's not ice cream weather at the moment, but it was beautiful in the summer and autumn.'

'I can see that I'll be doing a bit of exploring,' said Penny.

'I'd be happy to give you the initial tour, though I'm sure you could navigate it yourself,' he quickly added.

'I'll take you up on the offer of a tour.' She glanced at the storm rolling over the landscape, like dark blue ink being poured over the sky. 'On a bright day.'

'There will be plenty of those,' Neil assured her. 'We're fortunate that we're sheltered by the hills and mountains, tucked into this perfect little niche.'

'It really is a perfect place to stay,' she said, thinking how lucky she was.

Neil nodded, and for a moment he admired Penny, feeling that his world had improved even more from meeting her. Then he felt his heart jolt from thinking he'd like to ask her to go out to dinner with him. He'd learned from experience that sounding too eager too soon wasn't a good idea. Not that he had a lot of experience. Work had always taken precedence over romance, but that was something he wanted to change. At the very least, he liked Penny's company, and the fact that she was there with him watching the storm surely indicated that she liked his company too.

He folded the map and tucked it away again.

'What was the cabin like on the castle's estate, the one you stayed in when you came here for an artisan break?' she asked him.

'It was great, and more like a luxurious chalet than a wooden cabin. I could've stayed in the writer's cabin as that was available, but I opted for the artist's cabin instead. The writer's cabin had an antique desk and I considered staying there. Then I saw the artist's cabin had an area for painting, including easels and wonderful light coming in through the large window, and I thought it would be ideal for my goldwork.'

'So you set up your equipment in the cabin?'

'I brought the basic stuff. Mainly I was there for a break, to get away from the city, to see if I liked living in the Highlands.' He smiled and shrugged. 'And here I am.'

'Etta says a few residents started off by staying at the castle and now live here,' said Penny.

Neil agreed. 'Oliver, he's an artist. He came here for an artist's break at the castle cabin and now he's set up his shop in the main street. He's always got great paintings, oils and watercolours, in his shop window.'

'I've only glanced at it. The art shop is opposite the sweet shop.'

'Yes, and definitely worth a view. I don't really know Oliver, apart from being on nodding terms. He's around my age, single, if the gossip is true, and is secretly in love with one of the local ladies.'

'Which one?'

'I don't know. It's a secret. Or maybe just wild gossip.'

'I must have a look at Oliver's art shop window,' Penny said firmly. 'It's next to the flower shop, and I'd like a look in there.'

'It is. The flower shop is owned by yet another eligible man, Fyn. Or so I've heard. I don't know his story.'

'There's a great mix of shops in the main street. I didn't expect to find so many artisan and specialist businesses here.'

'Online shopping has been a game changer. The shops thrive from having websites and selling online, and it allows them to run profitable shops locally.'

'And provide more chances of romance, not that I'm looking to get involved at the moment,' she emphasised. 'But I must ask Etta about Oliver and Fyn. She knows all the gossip.'

Neil bit his lips, wishing he hadn't emphasised how eligible these new local men were. 'Did you enjoy your bee night?' he said, bringing the conversation back to the evening's event.

'I really did. I'm looking forward to the weekly get together at the castle. The members are so friendly and it's a lovely function room. And of course, we have tea and cake.'

'If I was into crafting, I'd join you,' he joked. 'But I seem to have found a handy way to keep my supply of jumpers and cardigans going.'

Penny glanced at the oven gloves in the back seat. 'Don't forget the oven gloves.'

Neil smiled. 'I've been meaning buy a pair, but never got around to searching for them online.'

'I think the ladies were happy that you were interested in their knitting and sewing.'

'That jumper Etta was knitting is exactly to my taste. Again, I've been so busy with work that I haven't got around to buying items that are suitable for cold days here.'

She looked at him sitting there in his expensive, well–cut shirt and trousers. 'I can't picture you as the casual dress type.'

'I'm not.' Then he frowned. 'Is that a bad thing?'

'No, the opposite. I like a man in a nice shirt.' Her eyes widened as she realised she'd said too much. 'What I mean is, an open neck shirt is the perfect compromise between smart and casual.'

'Don't feel embarrassed,' he said, seeing her blush. 'I'll take the compliment. I don't get too many of those.'

'I doubt that.'

'It's true.' His gorgeous blue eyes glanced over at her and she felt her heart thunder louder than the storm.

She pulled her attention back to the view. 'It looks like the rain is pouring down over there.'

A few specks of light rain were hitting off the car windscreen.

'Perhaps we'd better head home before it reaches full force,' he said.

Penny nodded. 'It looks like the storm is rolling this way.'

Neil turned the engine on, and then steered the car away from the parking area, driving them back down the hill towards their cottages.

The rain had increased by the time he pulled up outside Penny's cottage.

'Wait here,' he said, as she went to open the door to step out.

She waited.

Neil jumped out and grabbed an umbrella from the boot of the car, then ran round to open her door.

Penny smiled at him as he sheltered her.

She hurried to the front door of her cottage, dug her keys out from her craft bag and opened it. She couldn't remember any man being so chivalrous in a long time.

'Thank you, Neil.' She smiled warmly at him.

He stepped back, making it clear he wasn't angling for an invitation to come in. Take your time, he told himself, even though he wanted to join her to continue chatting to her over a cup of tea.

He sheltered under the umbrella, but the rain had already soaked the shoulders of his white shirt, and the fabric clung to his lean muscles, emphasising his fit build. 'Sleep tight. The cottages are sturdy and can weather the storm,' he assured her.

'Thanks for bringing me home.'

She watched him hurry back to his car, throw the umbrella in the boot, jump in and drive it the short distance to his own cottage. From her doorway she waved to him as he parked his car, grabbed the oven mitts and ran inside.

Penny glanced out at the rainy night. The cottage could weather the storm, but the same couldn't be said for the way her heart felt about Neil.

Neil stripped his wet shirt off and checked his messages. An email was waiting for him, an invitation from an important client, wanting to talk to him the next day over lunch to discuss another highly lucrative jewellery order.

He sighed and swithered what to do. The lunch meeting in Edinburgh wasn't the issue. He was happy to meet the client to secure a further deal, and trips to the city were part of his life. It would also give him a chance to visit his parents' restaurant. A visit to them was long overdue. Two birds, one stone, he told himself. No, none of this was an issue.

So, what was wrong? Why did he balk at the timing of it? The answer was — Penny.

He sighed again. He'd just got to know her, spent time with her, and he felt as if things would continue the next day. Now, he was off to Edinburgh, and he sensed it would jar their relationship's progress. Set things back a bit. The last thing he wanted. But he wasn't dating Penny, he reminded himself, or obliged to check in with her or tell her of his plans, even if it was only disappearing tomorrow without a word.

He rewound their time in the car watching the rain. She'd emphasised that she wasn't looking for romance at the moment. A subtle hint to him? Or aimed at the other local men he'd mentioned? He didn't know.

Checking the time, he realised it was far too late in the evening to pop round to her cottage on some excuse and bring up the topic that he'd be away on business. He'd have to leave at the crack of dawn to make it on time for the early lunch meeting, so chapping on her door before first light and wakening her up in the morning wasn't an option either.

He was stuck with his current predicament, he told himself resignedly.

Going through to his workshop, he flicked a lamp on and collected samples of goldwork pieces and sketches for the client to peruse. He put them in his briefcase and clicked it shut, ready to pick up in the morning.

The storm raged outside as he lay in bed and tried to get some sleep. He usually slept well, unless things were on his mind, and tonight there was one woman in his thoughts, as he went over the fun day and evening he'd enjoyed with Penny.

Penny felt two extremes — excited about her new friendship with Neil, and trepidation. Meeting Neil and feeling a strong attraction to him had upended her day. She'd meant what she'd said about not looking for romance at the moment. But saying it and adhering to it were two different things.

Unable to settle, she got out of bed, put her cardigan on over her cosy pyjamas, and padded through to the living room in her mended socks. She'd kept them on because the night was chilly.

Her pyjamas had patchwork repairs on them. She'd had them for years, along with a few other pairs, and all of them were mended to make them last. She loved her comfy jim–jams, and the colourful, cotton patches withstood being washed and worn. One day there would be more patch than original pyjama fabric, but she intended extending them, strengthening the seams, stitching any holes, adding strips of polka dot and ditsy print cotton fabric to the frayed hems, creating features of the edges.

She put the lamp on and sat down near the front window and picked up a piece of embroidery she'd been stitching. Mending, sewing, any type of stitching always relaxed her.

After several minutes of satin stitching a cornflower motif on to a top that needed mended and embellished, she went through to make a cup of tea in the kitchen.

Gazing out through the rain at the dark night, all she saw was her own uneasy face reflected in the window. While the kettle boiled, she opened the kitchen door and felt the rainy night sweep in. The cold air gusted past her into the cosy kitchen. She shut the door again quickly. A breath of fresh air tonight wasn't going to settle her this evening.

Prying open the biscuit tin, she picked up a piece of shortbread and took a bite. Midnight raids in the kitchen weren't a common occurrence, but her jangled senses warranted it.

She made a mug of tea and took it through to the living and sat down again to continue sewing. The room had retained the residual heat from the fire, and she felt cosy in her nightwear, fluffy slippers and cardigan.

The rhythmic stitches, the lovely colours of the thread, and the pretty floral design taking shape soothed her senses, and soon she was lost in her sewing, the one thing that always made her feel grounded and at home.

After an hour of embroidery mending, she went back to bed. The storm was still rumbling angrily outside the cottage, but she barely noticed it as she fell sound asleep and didn't stir until the morning.

Neil's car was gone the next morning. She noticed as she looked out the kitchen window while cooking porridge for breakfast.

She'd become accustomed to seeing his car tucked at the side of his garden fence every morning, though it disappeared occasionally at other times. Mainly though, Neil was a homebody like her. So if his car was gone, that meant Neil was gone. Not far, she assumed. He'd probably driven down to the wee shop for groceries. She'd eaten him out of house and home she thought, smiling to herself at the pancake and soufflé treats he'd cooked her.

The rain had stopped, but the grey sky bore an undertone that it could rain again soon. It would make sense to drive his car to the shops rather than risk getting soaked, especially if he'd been shopping for groceries.

Thinking no more of it, she started work. There was a lot of work to do, as always, but especially this morning as she'd skived off to the castle the previous night and spent more time with Neil than she'd planned. No complaints though. Not one. A few orders needed tackled, but she'd deal with those easily. Garments she'd artistically mended had been bought on her website and needed wrapped and taken later to the post office.

Her new designs needed tested too. All her designs, her embroidery patterns, were stitched to see if they needed tweaked and worked as she'd hoped.

She also planned to make a video showing herself stitching the new patterns, so after breakfast she set up her lighting and camera that she used for recording her videos at her sewing table.

She began by showing how she satin stitched the flower petals using single strands of cotton embroidery thread. Then she demonstrated her whipped back stitch for the stem, mixing two different shades of green thread. French knots filled the centres, and closed fly stitch created the leaves.

She replayed the video on her laptop and was relieved that it required very little editing. The lighting worked well and the close–up of the smooth, satin stitched petals looked lovely. So far, her new patterns worked well.

As lunch approached, she decided to have Scotch broth and a couple of slices of bread. She sat at the kitchen table enjoying her lunch and peered out the window. Neil's car was still gone. Maybe he'd been back home and gone again without her noticing. She'd been so busy doing the embroidery and voice–over on her video that she might not have heard him come and go.

It was the afternoon when she finally began to realise that Neil had gone. Without a word. No hint last night as he sheltered her under his umbrella from the rain that he'd be disappearing all day.

She shrugged off the feeling of being mildly miffed. Neil wasn't accountable to her. They weren't dating. No plans had been made for them to meet up today. So why did it unsettle her? The answer was simple. She liked Neil, and had assumed they'd continue their chatter and friendship today, maybe even this evening.

She sighed heavily. Her mistake.

Late in the afternoon, Penny walked down to the post office with her parcel orders. The previous night's rain had been absorbed into the lush landscape and heather, and the air felt extra fresh with the scent of greenery.

The parcels weren't heavy, so she didn't drive down. A walk to post office only took a few minutes, and she wanted to stroll along the main street and take a proper look at the art shop Neil had mentioned.

After dropping her parcels off, she walked the full length of the street, taking in all the different shops. The window of the sweet shop had a tempting selection of sweets, many of them old–fashioned recipes. Penny gave into temptation and went inside.

CHAPTER SEVEN

Sylvia smiled, pleased to see her. 'Penny! What can I get for you?'

Penny looked at all the sweets on display in the glass front counter and in jars on the shelves. 'I don't know. They all look so tempting. And something smells delicious.'

'My aunty is making Scottish tablet through in the back kitchen. A traditional recipe,' Sylvia explained, and showed Penny a tray of the tablet, cut into cubes like pieces of sweet and delicious fudge.

'I'll have some tablet,' said Penny. 'I haven't had tablet in ages.'

Sylvia popped a scoop of tablet in a bag and put it on the counter. 'Can I suggest you try a bag of our tasty mix.'

Penny frowned. 'What's that?'

'A wee bit of everything from our popular sweeties.'

'Yes, I'll try that.'

Sylvia took another paper bag and started picking one or two sweets from various selections. 'Cola cubes, Highland toffee, soor plooms, penny toffees, lemon sherbets, chocolate creams and a macaroon bar.' Sylvia added a few extras on the house.

Penny laughed as she paid for her sweets. 'You're spoiling me. I only came down to post my parcels and have a peek at the art shop.'

'Oliver's shop?'

'Yes, Neil mentioned it to me.'

'It's right over there.' She pointed out the front window at the white painted shop with paintings on display. Watercolours, oils and acrylics of local landscapes and floral paintings.

Penny peered out the window. 'Lovely paintings. Does Oliver paint them himself?'

'Yes, he's very talented, though I don't know him well. He nods over to me from time to time, and he's been in here a couple of times since I arrived.' She paused. 'He doesn't say much to me though. He's not like Bradoch at the bakery. Bradoch's always chatty.'

Penny lowered her voice. 'Neil says he's heard that Oliver is in love with one of the local ladies.'

'That's the rumour, but we've no idea if it's true. He arrived at Gaven's castle for an artist's break and stayed to open his own shop last summer.'

'So he's fairly new here too?'

'Yes, my aunt and Etta say there's never been so many young, eligible men here ever. They're opening wee shops and doing business online as well as local trade.'

'I think Oliver fancies Aileen,' Aunt Muira called through, overhearing the conversation.

'You could be right, Aunty,' Sylvia agreed. 'But Aileen says she hardly knows him either. He's never been in her quilt shop, but she did dance with him at the Christmas ceilidh. Most of us did. It was a fast–moving reel, so no opportunity to chat. Gaven's organising another ceilidh night soon, according to Jessy. She told me last night at the bee. You'll need to go to that. We all go to the party nights at the castle.'

'Sounds like fun,' Penny said, nodding.

'It is, and I reckon you'll have extra fun with Gaven.'

Penny frowned.

'Oh, don't pretend you didn't notice how interested Gaven is in you.'

Penny held up her hands. 'I'm really not planning to get wrapped up in romance so soon after arriving. I'm not properly settled yet.'

'Well, I'm just saying, I think you're lucky. Gaven is luscious.'

Her aunty giggled and continued to make the confectionary in the back kitchen.

'I heard that,' Sylvia called through to her.

'Gaven's very...handsome,' Penny admitted.

'He's double handsome!' Sylvia said firmly.

Penny smiled knowingly at her. 'So, you fancy the laird?'

'Most of the local ladies do. Imagine dating the laird and living in his castle...'

Penny thought about it for a moment and nodded.

'Especially as Gaven's tall, dark and handsome,' Sylvia added. 'I wish he looked at me the way he was looking at you last night.'

Penny brushed this comment aside. 'I'm the shiny new thing. The novelty will wear off soon.'

'Hmmm, maybe, but he had a definite glint in his eyes,' said Sylvia. 'And you've certainly dazzled Neil.'

'I'm just friends with Neil.'

Sylvia put her hands on her hips. 'I'm not buying it. I think you like him, if you know what I mean.'

Penny sighed and kept her voice down. 'Okay, so I kind of like Neil, but I'm not getting involved with him. It's too soon. I barely know him.'

'He fed you twice yesterday and took you for a romantic drive in the rain to the kissing spot up on the hill.'

'How did you know...?' Penny shook her head. 'Gossip travels at the speed of light around here.'

Sylvia kept her voice down. 'Did Neil kiss you? Did you give in to temptation?'

'No! We talked about the weather, about other things...and he showed me his map of the area. He's offered to take me on a tour, including a trip to the cove on the coast.'

Sylvia laughed.

Penny frowned. 'What?'

'I think that could be considered a date.'

'It's not a date.'

'It's a date,' Aunt Muira chimed–in from the kitchen.

Penny gave in. 'Okay, so it's sort of, but not really a date, a day out, with Neil.' Then she asked. 'Do you know where Neil is today?'

'Working in his cottage I would think,' said Sylvia.

'No. His car was gone early this morning, before I'd had breakfast, and he hasn't been there all day,' Penny explained.

'I've no idea. Didn't Neil tell you where he was going?'

'No, but why should he, we're not involved.'

'You sound miffed,' Sylvia surmised.

'I'm not,' Penny lied. 'I just wonder where he's gone. He never mentioned anything to me last night. I assumed I'd see him in the morning.'

'For more home cooked pancakes?' Sylvia teased her.

Penny smiled. 'I guess I'll see him when I see him.'

'Enjoy your sweeties,' Sylvia said to her. 'They'll keep you sweet until Neil comes home.'

Penny put the confectionary in her bag, shrugged it up on her shoulder, headed out, and crossed the road to have a look in the art shop window.

There was no sign of Oliver, and she took the chance to stand there and admire the paintings on view. The vibrant blues, yellows, pinks and greens of the modern floral watercolours were gorgeous, and so different to the oil and acrylic paintings that depicted the local landscape in a traditional style. She was trying to decide what she preferred when a man's voice spoke over her shoulder.

'Sorry, I just popped to the wee shop for milk,' the man said to her, holding up the milk and a set of keys to open the shop. 'I don't usually have customers this late in the day.'

Penny took in the tall, fine featured man with a shock of dark brown hair and green eyes. He wore jeans and a denim shirt with the sleeves rolled up to reveal whipcord forearms. The speckles of paint on his hands and the shirt indicated that this was Oliver.

His voice was filled with inflection, polite and yet friendly, and his warm smile and open nature made her feel comfortable following him into his shop.

'I don't want to waste your time,' she said quickly. 'I was just having a look at the paintings in your window.'

'You're Penny, aren't you?'

Penny blinked. 'Eh, yes.'

'I try to learn the names of the newcomers,' he explained. 'Come in and have a look around. I don't expect you to buy anything.'

Her senses eased and again she felt comfortable in his presence, as if he meant what he said.

He put the milk through in the kitchen at the back of the shop.

'Are you an artist yourself?' he asked her.

'No, not like this, painting watercolours and oils. I design patterns for creative mending and embroidery patterns.'

'Creative mending? For clothes?'

'Yes, and other items.' She explained briefly about her business.

He unhooked one of his aprons, a white apron splattered with watercolour paint. 'Could you patch the pockets on this apron? I ripped it the other day and sewing isn't my thing. It's a fairly new apron, not that you could tell from the state of it covered in watercolour splatters, but I like to get a lot of use from my aprons. I tore it on my workbench. It's been washed. Could you mend it?'

'Yes, I could repair it for you.' She took the clean, but watercolour stained, apron from him and explained the options. 'I could replace the pockets with colourful patchwork pockets, but perhaps you don't want anything too colourful.'

'No, knock yourself out. My world is filled with colour. The more the better, except when it's the landscapes. Folk prefer those to be subtle.'

'I'll take it with me.' She folded the apron and put it in her bag.

He caught a glimpse of the confectionery. 'That's a lot of tasty sweeties you've got there.'

She glanced over at the sweet shop. 'Sylvia's been lavish and letting me try a selection of the sweets they sell. The shop smells delicious.'

Oliver looked over at the shop. 'Do you know Sylvia?'

'Yes, she's one of the members of the crafting bee. The ladies were up at the castle last night.' She elaborated about their evening.

Oliver folded his strong, lean arms across his chest and leaned back on the counter. His green eyes flickered with interest in everything she was telling him.

'Gaven's the local heartthrob, or so I've heard from the gossip,' said Oliver.

Penny shrugged. 'He's the laird and lives in a castle. He's tall, dark and handsome. He's a lot of ladies fairytales come true.'

Oliver nodded thoughtfully. 'Some men have all the luck.'

'Gaven must be doing something wrong,' said Penny. 'He's not dating any of them, and he's always busy running the castle and the estate.'

Oliver smiled broadly. 'I like your attitude, Penny. Fancy a cup of tea? I'll exchange you a cuppa for a piece of that tablet or macaroon bar.'

'Deal,' Penny said firmly.

They laughed as Oliver went through and put the kettle on for tea.

She wandered around the shop, admiring the paintings. 'I love your work.'

'Thanks, what do you take in your tea?' he called through to her.

'Just milk.'

She heard him making the tea, opened her bag and took the tablet and macaroon bar through to him. 'Help yourself.'

Oliver was washing his hands at the sink. He dried them and turned around. 'The macaroon bar looks tasty.'

'Half each,' she said. 'And take a couple of pieces of tablet.'

Oliver helped himself and popped a square of tablet in his mouth. 'It melts perfectly,' he mumbled.

Penny laughed, and admired the kitchen, especially the beautiful blue and white tiles on the walls near the sink. He'd painted a tall wooden dresser eau–de–nil, and it held an eclectic mix of dinner plates and jars of watercolour brushes. Vintage teacups sat beside a matching teapot. Porcelain mugs that he'd hand–painted with flowers, butterflies and bees hung on hooks.

Oliver noticed her interest. 'The tiles are part of the original decor.'

'They're lovely. I like vintage decor.'

'Most of the shops in the main street are the authentic buildings from the past. They're all sturdily built, each a slightly different design. I live above the shop, as do quite a few others in the main street, or they live at the back of the shop. Everyone seems to have kept as much of the original style as possible. I love that. I like that the past styling isn't totally swept aside in favour of new stuff.'

Penny admired the old–fashioned looking cooker.

'The cooker is new but has a vintage vibe,' he explained. 'The two big butler sinks are from years ago. I use one for my work, washing brushes and water jars, and the other for clean, domestic use.'

Penny looked at the two sinks and tried not to smile. There were a few splatters of watercolour paint on the clean sink.

Oliver grinned. 'I try to anyway.'

He made two mugs of tea, and they sat down on wooden stools he'd painted robin egg blue to chat and eat the sweets.

She told him about her circumstances in moving from the city and living in the cottage.

'The cottages are idyllic,' he said. 'But it's cosy and convenient living above my art shop. Maybe, in the future, if I marry and settle down, I'll move to a cottage or one of the farmhouse conversions.'

Penny ate her half of the macaroon bar while listening to him talk about his artwork.

He pulled his laptop over on to the kitchen table and opened it. 'What's your business called?'

She explained that her website was under her name as he searched and found it online. 'But I'm thinking of calling it Sewing and Mending Cottage.'

Oliver was now scrolling through her website and nodding at the pictures of her mending work and patterns. 'Beautiful work. I like that you've made the mending look artistic, a feature of the repairs. The colours you've used are wonderful. Colour is definitely my thing.'

'Except for the subtle tones of your landscapes.'

'Yes,' he said, and then smiled. 'But there's really nothing subtle about me.'

Penny nodded. Oliver was such a bright character.

Their conversation wound full circle back to the local gossip.

'I suppose you'll have heard the rumour about me being secretly in love with one of the local girls,' he said.

'I have. Sylvia's aunt thinks it's Aileen.'

Oliver frowned. 'The owner of the quilt shop?' His tone indicated that it wasn't Aileen he'd a crush on.

'So the rumour is true,' Penny surmised.

'It might be.'

'But it's not Aileen.'

He shook his head.

She didn't push him any further and changed the conversation. 'Neil, the goldsmith, mentioned that you stayed in one of the cabin's at the castle.'

'I did. I came to paint the landscapes, get away from the city, and have a wee working holiday,' he explained. 'I loved the community, and decided to move here. This shop was available so I took it. Folk were so welcoming to me as a newcomer. Then later on, Sylvia arrived, and now the newly minted one is you.'

'Etta says it keeps the community lively.'

'It certainly does,' Oliver agreed.

'Sylvia told me that Gaven is planning a ceilidh night at the castle soon.' She thought she'd tell him. If the woman he liked was local there was a fair chance she'd be there, so this would give him a chance to dance with her.

'I thought there wouldn't be another ceilidh for a wee while.' He smiled. 'But I'm up for that. I like to dance and have fun.'

She didn't doubt it.

The shop's doorbell tinkled indicating that a last minute customer had come in.

'I'd better go,' said Penny. 'Thanks for the tea.'

'Nice to get to know you, Penny.' He hurried through to deal with the customer.

Penny left him another two pieces of tablet and a share of the sweets on a plate on the kitchen table. Then smiling, she went through to the front shop, nodded acknowledgment to the customer, a man she'd never met, waved to Oliver and went on her way.

The sky was darkening as she walked back to her cottage. A deep, inky blue and amber twilight stretched across the landscape, but there was no hint of rain in the air. No hint of Neil either. His car wasn't there.

She went inside her cottage and took Oliver's apron out of her bag. Her mind was already planning how to repair it, and as she wasn't feeling hungry for dinner having eaten sweets and downed a mug of tea, she set about working on it in her living room.

After lighting the fire and hearing it spark into life, she put the lamps on and sat in the cosy glow to look through her fabric stash. The apron was a good quality cotton, and she had lovely quilting weight cotton scraps to create the pockets. This would give an even more artistic design to the apron. She looked at the ditsy prints, florals and polka dots and then decided to opt for solid colours — vibrant turquoise, aqua green, golden yellow, cherry red and heliotrope. Colours that she'd seen in Oliver's floral watercolours in his art shop window.

She played around with the design until she was happy with it. An artistic geometric pattern with bold colours. Measuring his existing pockets, she cut the new fabric to size and used her sewing machine to make the pockets and then stitch them on to the apron.

Holding it up, she liked the effect she'd created. She'd also strengthened the corners of the pockets with extra stitching. It would make them last longer. Happy with her work, and hoping Oliver would be happy too, she pressed the apron and hung it up on the rail of garments at the far end of the living room.

By now the day had darkened to early evening and she was ready for her dinner.

She went through to the kitchen, peeled and boiled a pot of hearty vegetables and a pot of potatoes. The local vegetables were delicious. It was a treat having them freshly cooked and served with a tasty cheese sauce sprinkled with chives.

She'd just finished her dinner, cleared things away in the kitchen, and was aiming to settle down for an evening of sewing.

But a knock on the front door changed her plan for a cosy night.

She peered out the window before opening the door, and was surprised to see the tall figure of a man wearing an expensive looking dark leisure jacket standing there. For a moment, she thought it was Neil. But no. It was Gaven.

Penny opened the door wearing a pale blue jumper, grey jeans and a pair of beige pumps. The night air blew in and she stood aside. 'Gaven! Come on in.'

He stepped inside and she closed the door to keep the cold air out. His tall stature made the hall seem smaller, and she was aware how good looking he was.

'I never got a chance to give you that tour of the castle,' he began before she could ask him if something was wrong. He glanced into the living room, feeling the warmth from the fire and the glow from the lamps.

'The cottage is looking lovely,' he said, distracted, because Penny was looking lovely too.

'It's a pretty cottage. I've settled in nicely.'

'Anyway,' he continued. 'I wondered if you'd like to come up this evening, for a tour, and perhaps stay for supper.'

Was Gaven asking her to have a date with him? It certainly sounded like a date.

'There are no hidden motives,' he told her. 'We never got a chance to chat last night with all the fuss and furore.'

Like a moth to flame, she found herself nodding and taking Gaven up on his invitation.

An evening with the laird, with the promise of no hidden motives, was hard to resist. She could sew any night she wanted, but a tour of the castle and supper with the laird was something she'd no reason to refuse.

CHAPTER EIGHT

Gaven's dark, all–terrain car was parked outside Penny's cottage. The night was brisk, but dry, so thinking she'd only be going to his car and then to the castle, she secured the cottage, put her jacket on, picked up her bag and followed him outside. She didn't wear her warm boots and kept her beige pumps on which she thought would be better for touring the castle. Trudging around the beautiful rooms in the castle wearing furry boots wasn't necessary.

Gaven drove them off, looking like a man whose evening was going to plan.

The drive was a short one to the castle, and they'd barely exchanged casual pleasantries before he was driving through the entrance. But instead of heading to the front door of the castle, he veered off to the left, taking the narrow and tree arched road that led to the luxury cabins and holiday cottages.

'I thought we'd start with a look inside one of the cabins,' Gaven said before she could ask him where they were going.

This area of the estate had taken the brunt of the recent rainstorm, soaking up the downpour, and patches of the ground were still damp.

Solar lamps lit the contours of the road, as did the car's headlights. Cabins with their windows aglow, and cottages likewise further down the banking near the river, looked like they were situated in a timeless setting. The greenery and trees dotted with lamps looked like a magical forest.

'The cabins look fairly new,' Penny remarked.

'They're a recent addition to the estate,' Gaven explained. 'Originally, I wanted to use the cottages for the artisan breaks, self–catering retreats for writers, artists, creatives seeking a working holiday away from the city, the hubbub, where they could relax and create at their leisure. My idea was that the cottages would be part of the castle's facilities while being apart from it, if you know what I mean.'

Penny nodded.

'But the cottages weren't quite ideal for artisan breaks where more room was required, large windows to let in lots of daylight for artists, writers' desks with extra space for lounging. The cottages are traditional, and they're still used for self–catering retreats, but three years ago I decided to have the cabins custom built. The bookings took off and have been very successful. We've had writers, artists, and others coming to the retreats.'

'A few of them have stayed, and opened businesses, like Oliver with his art shop,' said Penny.

'Yes, including your new friend and acquaintance, the goldsmith.'

Gaven's tone was laced with a hint of jealousy, unless she was mistaken, which she doubted.

'It's surely been a boost to the local community to have the shops in the main street thriving with new businesses.'

'It's been a tremendous boost,' Gaven agreed. 'Some of the shops had become shadows of their former selves, and now they're busy with online sales as well as local trade.'

'I'm lucky to be able to run my business from my cottage.'

Gaven smiled. 'While still having time to visit the castle and enjoy an evening excursion to a fairytale forest.'

'You're a bad influence on me,' she scolded him lightly. 'I should be working.'

'You're always sewing late into the twilight hours. You're entitled to a night off for bad behaviour.'

'Don't you mean good behaviour?'

He smiled at her. 'You're the one that said I was a bad influence on you.'

'I already had a night off for the bee evening,' she said.

'You got some sewing done,' he argued.

'I did, and I worked into the wee small hours when I got back to the cottage.'

'Then you're definitely due some fun.'

He pulled up outside one of the luxury cabins. It was in darkness. He turned the engine off, dug into his jacket pocket and then dangled a set of keys. 'The new resident doesn't arrive until tomorrow, so I'll let you see inside. This cabin is kitted out with easels and tables suitable for an artist to paint, and a drawing desk for sketching.'

The path up to the cabin was wet, and the greenery looked damp and sparkled with rain.

Penny hesitated and glanced at her nice beige pumps. Typical! The one time she could've done with her boots.

'Ah,' Gaven said, seeing the predicament. 'I don't want you to ruin your shoes. I should've told you to wear boots.' But he'd been so anxious, hoping she'd accept his invitation that he hadn't thought about her shoes.

'It's okay,' she said, thinking she could clean them, even though they would probably be stained from walking across the wet and slightly muddy ground.

'No. Hold on,' he insisted, and jumped out of the car.

He ran round to the passenger side, opened her door and smiled. 'Put your arm around my shoulders.' He leaned in to pick her up.

'Really, it's okay. The shoes aren't worth the trouble—'

'It's no trouble, Penny. Come on.'

Without any help from her, she found herself lifted up in his strong arms and being carried over the wet path to the front door of the cabin.

'Fish the keys from my pocket,' he instructed. 'I can't reach them while holding you.'

She felt the urge to laugh, but suppressed it, until she had to rummage in his jacket pocket trying to find the key.

'This is becoming a trend with us,' she said, giggling. 'Where's the key?'

'Try the other pocket.'

She did.

By now he was the one trying to contain his laughter.

'If anyone is watching us, this looks bad,' she told him, finally finding the key.

'Remember the golden rule.'

'What's that?' she said, opening the door while still in his arms.

'There's always someone watching, even in the wilds of the Scottish Highlands, at night.'

He stepped inside the cabin and didn't immediately put her down.

'You can put me down now, Gaven,' she said calmly, while her heart thundered in her chest.

He put her down and closed the cabin door.

'Call it practice.' He turned the lights on, creating a warm glow to the main room of the cabin.

'Practice for what?' she said, starting to wander around, eager to see the equipment and layout of the cabin.

'For being carried over the threshold.'

'Huh! I'd need to find a husband first for that, and I'm not even in the dating game right now.'

'No?'

She turned to face him. 'No, definitely not.'

A knock on the cabin door startled them.

Penny stared at Gaven.

Gaven shrugged, and then opened the door to find Walter standing there. He had a box filled with logs and kindling for the fire.

'Sorry to disturb your canoodling,' Walter apologised.

'We weren't canoodling,' Penny called over to him as Gaven hesitated to refute Walter's assumption.

Walter smiled tightly, clearly unconvinced. 'I'll leave the logs here. I brought them over to stock the cabin ready for the new guest arriving in the morning.' He put the box down.

'Thank you, Walter,' Gaven told him in a voice that was appreciative, but urging him to get lost.

Walter got the message, and scarpered.

Gaven closed the door again.

Penny sighed. She could just picture the gossip trail being lit like touch paper.

'Walter will be discreet,' Gaven lied.

Penny glared at him.

'Okay, so we're going to be the topic of gossip, but it doesn't matter.'

'Maybe not to you, but I've still not become accustomed to being talked about.'

'There would be a bit of gossip anyway because of me giving you the tour tonight,' he said.

'Don't you do this for all new residents in the community?'

The look he gave her. That would be a no.

'For most of them?' she said.

Another no.

'A few of them would be more accurate,' he told her. 'I thought with you being artistic, and at the bee night anyway, you would've liked to see around the castle. But, of course, it didn't work out so handily.'

She nodded. That was a fair assessment.

He took a deep breath and proceeded to show her the cabin. 'The lighting includes daylight bulbs to allow artists to work in the evenings.' He walked over to the large window that had a view of the forest. 'Plenty of daylight streams in and artists have commented that the atmosphere is great for creativity.'

'I'm sure it is. I'd happily sit here and sew. It feels cosy and calm. But I'm fortunate that my cottage provides that type of atmosphere.'

'So you think you'll settle here in our community?'

'I do. I love it.'

'Even when you're the topic of gossip?'

'That will wear off when the next newcomer is in the main spotlight.'

'True,' he agreed. 'For the moment, people are going to be chattering about us.'

'Walter probably saw you carrying me into the cabin,' she said.

'There's no probably about it.' He smiled at her. 'Come on, I'll carry you back to the car and show you around the castle.'

Turning the lights off and locking the cabin door, Gaven lifted Penny up and carried her to the car.

Penny started giggling.

'What are you laughing at?' he said, placing her carefully into the passenger seat.

'You. I bet you had a whole different plan for this evening.'

He got into the driver's side and started up the engine. 'I did. I planned to show you the cabin, without having to lift you up into my arms again.' He frowned thoughtfully. 'But I prefer the alternative plan. I'm glad you didn't wear your boots.'

She threw him a scolding look.

His grey–green eyes glanced at her. 'You want me to lie?'

'Yes, probably, maybe, sort of.'

'I'm glad you're so sure about that.'

Penny laughed, and Gaven joined in, and their laughter was apparent to anyone watching as he drove them up to the front entrance of the castle. The double doors were open and the warmth of the castle's reception shone out into the night. The light reflected off the damp ground and a few puddles.

'Scuppered again,' he said, unable to park for other cars belonging to guests taking up the spaces. He stopped his car as near as possible to the entrance, and then glanced at her shoes. 'You know what I'm going to have to do now, don't you?'

Penny smiled and nodded.

Gaven went round to the passenger side and lifted Penny from the car.

As he carried her the short distance to the front entrance, she smiled at him. 'We're becoming adept at this, aren't we?'

'It'll save me having a workout later on before going to bed.' Then he took her by surprise as he lifted her up, as if she was a barbell and pressed her upwards, pretending to use her as a training method. He pumped her up and down a couple of times.

'No, Gaven!' she screamed, while laughing at the same time.

Guests were having dinner in the function room and the bar restaurant, and a few were checking in or out at the reception desk. Numerous faces stared amused and curious as Gaven walked past reception and into his office with Penny in his arms.

Nudging the door shut, he then put her down beside his desk.

'That's how to make an entrance,' he said jokingly.

'You're the most troublesome man I've ever met,' she scolded him, laughing at his antics.

'Oliver's a rascal. Don't let his friendly artist facade fool you. And you haven't danced at a ceilidh with Bradoch our baker, or Fyn.'

'I haven't even met Fyn. He owns the flower shop, doesn't he?'

'He does. My antics pall into insignificance compared to them.'

Penny frowned. 'Oliver doesn't seem like a rascal. He gave me a cup of tea. We discussed our work and he asked me to mend his artists' apron, and I have. Bradoch is always so cheery. No rascal tendencies that I've observed.'

'Trust me. I'm well behaved in comparison to some of them, at least according to me.'

'What about Neil? He's not a troublemaker.'

'No, Neil is extremely well behaved. Not that I'm insinuating he's boring.'

'He's gone off today. Do you know where he is?'

'No idea. Perhaps he should've told you, considering he drove you to the kissing spot last night.'

'You heard?'

'Everybody heard. Neil isn't inclined to romantic gestures, not that we've seen. But perhaps you've brought that out in him.'

A panicked knock on the door interrupted their conversation, and the castle's head chef, a man in his forties, wearing whites and a chef's hat at an anxious tilt, came barging in.

'The haggis went on fire when I scorched the flaming whisky sauce, but we've turned the alarm off,' the chef blurted out. 'Sorry to interrupt your canoodling with Penny, but now I'll have to change tonight's menu. Is Lorne sausage, tatties and neeps with gravy okay with you, Gaven?'

Seemingly used to his chef's attitude, Gaven replied calmly. 'Yes, cook what you see fit. Lorne sausage, tatties and neeps sounds tasty.'

'I'll add a sprinkling of greentails,' the chef said as he hurried away.

Penny smiled and a momentary calm allowed her to look around Gaven's office. Traditional wood panelling and a plush burgundy carpet enriched the decor. An antique desk dominated the room, making the modern laptop sitting on it somewhat out of place. In the hub of the castle, the office had a vintage writing bureau and filing cabinets from yesteryear that appeared to be still in use.

'It's old–fashioned, but I wanted to retain the original quality of the furnishings,' Gaven explained.

'I love it,' Penny told him. 'If it wasn't for the computer, this would be the perfect set for an old–fashioned drama series.'

'There's always plenty of drama around here,' said Gaven.

A moment later, Jessy knocked and hurried in. 'There's a skirmish in the bar restaurant. Could you come and sort it out?'

'Can't Walter handle the troublemakers?'

Jessy took a steadying breath. 'Walter's one of them.'

With a heavy sigh, but in no rush, Gaven excused himself and followed Jessy out of the office.

Unable to contain her curiosity, Penny hurried after them instead of waiting in the office.

'Is there usually bar brawls in the castle?' Penny whispered to Jessy as they scurried past reception.

'No, there's rarely any fisticuffs or argy–bargy here,' Jessy assured her. 'Guests are always well–mannered.'

'What's the disagreement about?' Penny asked quickly as they went into the bar restaurant. The sound of raised voices, one of them Walter's, resonated in anger.

'About you and Gaven,' Jessy stated, giving Penny a knowing look. 'People saw you and the laird getting frisky in the forest, then disappearing into one of the cabins.'

'We weren't up to anything untoward,' Penny told her, giving her the shortened version of events.

Jessy tugged her hand–knitted lilac cardigan around her. 'No one blames you for having the hots for the laird.'

'I don't have the hots for Gaven!' Penny shouted.

Her remark silenced the arguing, and she blushed as all the faces in the room looked directly at her.

'Anybody want a plate of sausage, tatties and neeps?' the head chef called into the room. 'With greentails.'

Penny decided to take action, feeling frowned on, in the spotlight, the focus of gossip, scandalous behaviour and mischief.

Unconcerned about ruining her nice shoes, she ran from the room, through reception and out into the night. The ground wasn't as wet as she'd thought and she jumped the puddles, taking the racing line out of the castle gates.

Picking up speed, she ran down the narrow road that led to her cottage. The downward slope added to her momentum, and there was a benefit in wearing flat shoes. She could run in them. She'd been planning to go for a run near the loch, so here she was, just not quite as she'd imagined.

Car headlights caught up with her, illuminating her in the main beam.

Feeling like a fugitive from some movie she'd watched in the past, she put on a spurt of speed and tried to use evasive action, darting off the road on to the grass and heather. The heather felt quite bouncy to run on and added a spring to her steps.

Gaven opened the car window and shouted to her. 'Penny. Stop. Slow down. I want to talk to you. I want to apologise.'

But something in Penny, a flicker of determination, a streak of stubbornness, made her ignore him and do what she wanted. And that was to get home to her cottage and lock the door to the world.

She'd almost made it, and would have if Gaven hadn't abandoned the car near her cottage and make a fast bolt to cut her off at the pass.

She ran into his extended arms.

'Penny, wait, stop. Let me explain.'

Penny's breath filtered into the brisk night air, but she was fitter than she thought. Part of her was happy that she hadn't lost any of her running ability, her speed.

'You're a fast runner,' Gaven said, holding her shoulders, keeping a grip of her, and trying to make her listen.

'If I'd had my training shoes on, I'd have made it to the cottage before you.' She looked up at him in defiance.

Gaven smiled.

'What?' she said, looking up, challenging him.

'You're beautiful when you're angry.'

'That's not a compliment.'

'Yes, it is,' he told her. His warm smile started to ease her senses.

She took a steadying breath and calmed down. 'Thank you for the attempted tour of your castle. I'd like to say it was fun, but I hate lying.'

He grinned at her. 'You had some fun. Come on, even just a little.'

She felt a smile rise inside her. 'Relaxing with my sewing and embroidery is fun. Mending, that's fun too. I like to cook, especially baking cakes. I enjoy that. But tonight's fiasco at the castle, starting with accusations of canoodling at the cabin, culminating in getting frisky in the forest, aren't my idea of a fun time.'

'You're smiling, Penny.'

'I'm not.' She tried not to.

'Just a little bit.'

She smiled a little bit, and then gave in. 'Okay, so that was sort of crazy wild. Definitely one for the archives.'

'Thank you for accepting my invitation to the castle.'

'My pleasure,' she lied.

'That was a lie,' he said.

'Yes.' The crispness in her tone matched the brisk night air.

He took a deep breath. 'Okay, I'd better get back to the castle.' He smiled and headed to his car, got in and started to drive away.

Penny unlocked her cottage door and watched him drive off.

Then she went inside and closed the door firmly against the world, knowing that she was in for another restless night.

She got ready for bed, but didn't go to it. Instead, she made a cup of tea, ate a cola cube and a piece of tablet from the sweetie bag, and sat in the living room sewing, mending and relaxing into the early hours, before heading to bed to get some sleep.

CHAPTER NINE

'Stand beside your counter and hold your buns up,' Oliver instructed Bradoch.

Penny walked into the bakery mid–morning the following day, after having dropped off a couple of parcel orders to the post office.

Oliver focussed through the lens of his camera as Bradoch adjusted the height of his sticky buns.

'Is this better?' Bradoch asked Oliver.

'Yes.' Oliver clicked the camera, taking a couple of photos and then checked the images. 'This should work nicely. Just a few more, and then I'll let you get back to serving your customers.'

Penny paused, wondering whether to leave and come back, stand and wait, or sit down and join Etta, Sylvia and Robin at their table where gossip was being exchanged over tea and scones.

'I've put an oatmeal loaf aside for you, Penny,' Bradoch told her, while standing at the counter wearing his whites. 'Grab a cup.' He indicated the cups beside the teapots.

Penny picked up a cup and joined the ladies. 'What's Oliver doing taking photographs of Bradoch?'

Etta poured her a cup of tea and smiled, keen to discuss the gossip.

'Oliver is creating a set of paintings of some of the shops in the main street,' Etta explained. 'Bradoch has agreed that his bakery will be one of them. Oliver wants the owners of the shops in the paintings. He's taking pictures so he can sketch the bakery and Bradoch when he gets back to his art shop.'

Penny sipped her tea. 'There are a lot of pretty shops in the main street. I'm sure he'll be spoiled for choice which ones to paint.'

'He's including the wee shop with the grocer, Aileen's quilt shop, Fyn's flower shop and a few others including the post office with the postmaster,' said Etta.

Sylvia finished drinking her tea. 'I'm going to tell my aunty what Oliver's doing. He's bound to want to paint the sweet shop — with me posing in the painting.' Sylvia struck a pose and giggled. 'I'll see you later.'

Penny noticed that Oliver kept glancing over at their table, not looking at her or Etta. She figured he was watching Sylvia, but when she stood up and left the bakery, Oliver's focus didn't waver. Penny realised it wasn't Sylvia that Oliver was interested in, it was Robin.

'I heard Oliver tell Bradoch he's been commissioned to do the paintings as artwork prints for a home decor company,' said Robin. 'I had a commission like that last year for my textile art, for wall prints. It was handy money.' Robin then tucked into her buttered scone, while Oliver showed the photos he'd taken to Bradoch.

Etta grinned at Penny. 'And I heard you were canoodling with the laird last night.'

Penny sighed and explained what really happened.

'You ran home?' Etta gasped. 'What did Gaven do?'

'He drove after me and caught up just as I'd reached my cottage,' Penny told her.

Robin laughed. 'I'd have loved to have seen that.'

Penny sighed and shook her head. 'I knew you'd all be gossiping about me.'

'Jessy phoned me,' said Etta. 'She told me that Gaven carried you into his office. Did he take you upstairs to his private turret?'

'No, only his office, which is so classy,' said Penny. 'Then there was the whole kerfuffle in the bar restaurant.'

'Jessy says that Walter was only defending your honour,' Etta insisted. 'He'd mentioned to the bar staff about you and Gaven being cosy in the cabin. One of the guests drinking in the bar caused the trouble to spark by making an inappropriate remark about what the two of you were up to.'

Penny's shoulders slumped. 'I wouldn't even have gone with Gaven for a tour of his castle if I'd known it wasn't common practise.'

Robin smiled at Penny. 'It's obvious that Gaven's interested in you.'

'I'm not getting involved with the laird,' Penny told them.

Etta wasn't convinced. 'We'll see.'

By now, Oliver had finished taking pictures of Bradoch and came over to their table. Although he spoke to all three of them, Penny noticed that his interest was in Robin. He seemed almost shy, and unable to say what was really on his mind.

'Come on, Oliver, show us the pictures,' Etta encouraged him.

Oliver was happy to let her see the images on his camera.

'The bakery looks beautiful,' Etta remarked.

'Bradoch will make a great character to paint,' said Oliver. 'I'm adding one person to each painting. It's the outside of the shops that I'm painting, but I wanted to capture Bradoch with a tray of buns, and with it being such a blustery day, I took the pictures inside the bakery.'

Penny, Etta and Robin viewed the photos, agreeing that the bakery would look lovely as a painting.

'I've included his sandwich board with the day's specials,' Oliver pointed out to them. 'I'm going to add that to the painting — soda scones, tea bread, sticky buns, Scottish fruit loaf and chocolate cake. I'll have Bradoch standing beside it I think.'

'I wish I could draw people,' said Robin. 'My textile art is mainly landscapes and other scenes, but not people. I've never been skilled at figurative art.'

'It just takes practise,' Oliver said to Robin. He wanted to offer to show Robin handy techniques for drawing figures, but Bradoch interrupted their conversation.

'I'm quite excited about my bakery shop being part of your new artwork collection,' Bradoch told Oliver. 'And I'll be in it. I hope I'll be able to buy a copy.'

'I'll make sure you get one,' Oliver promised him.

Bradoch smiled. 'Cheers, Oliver.'

Penny stood up, getting ready to buy her oatmeal loaf and then leave. 'I've a lot of sewing to catch up on.'

'That's what happens when you get chased by the laird,' Etta said jokingly.

Penny laughed. 'Don't remind me.'

Penny paid for her oatmeal bread, succumbed to a chocolate loaf too, and then headed out.

Oliver left with Penny, leaving Etta and Robin in the bakery.

'Are you going to include the sweet shop?' Penny said as they walked along together.

Oliver frowned. 'I'd love to paint the sweet shop, but there's a problem.'

'What's that?'

'I'm only including one figure and one shop in each painting. That's what the art brief has been agreed on.'

Penny didn't see the problem. 'Sylvia will be happy to pose outside the sweet shop.'

Oliver's frown deepened. 'I'd prefer to paint her Aunt Muira. She has the perfect look for the painting. Sylvia is beautiful, but she's not right for the scene. Muira is my choice, especially when she wears that cute, old fashioned hat when she's making the confectionery.'

Penny understood his predicament. Sylvia would be disappointed not to be included, and that Oliver had chosen her aunt over her.

'I could talk to Sylvia—'

'No, I should do it, but I just haven't found the right moment.'

'You will.'

Oliver nodded. 'I'll probably go there now.'

Penny dug into her bag and handed him the apron she'd mended. 'I hope you like the colours and the design.'

Oliver couldn't wait to see what she'd done and unfolded it. He held it up and smiled. 'This is fantastic. I love it.'

Penny was pleased. 'I'm glad you're happy.'

'If I bought another two new white aprons, would you give them a makeover like this?'

'Yes, I'll do that for you,' she assured him.

'I'm going to have my photo taken to promote an art feature in a magazine, and I need a new picture of myself for my website. I'd love to wear an apron like this.'

'I could exchange the white straps for colourful ones as well as adding a dash of colour to the pockets,' Penny suggested.

'I'll order the aprons today and then let you work your creative stitching on them.' He sounded excited.

'Okay, let me know when they arrive and I'll do that,' Penny told him.

Waving happily, Oliver walked on towards the sweet shop, while Penny headed back to her cottage.

She'd almost arrived, when she noticed that Neil's car was parked at the side of his cottage. Her heart soared, taking her aback at how pleased she was that he was home.

He must have seen her walking by, because his front door opened and he stepped outside into the morning sunlight.

Neil smiled at Penny, looking as pleased to see her as she was to see him.

He came striding over to her cottage, dressed smartly in a shirt, waistcoat and trousers that were part of a dark suit.

Her heart reacted as he walked right up to her, those gorgeous pale blue eyes gazing down at her.

'You're home,' she said. 'I wondered where you'd gone.' She made no attempt to hide that she'd been missing him.

'Edinburgh, on business. I received a message after dropping you off at your cottage. It was so late that I didn't want to disturb you, and I left at the crack of dawn. I doubled the trip with a visit to my parents' restaurant. I stayed with them a little longer than I'd initially intended.'

Penny listened to Neil's explanation, understanding his motives for not telling her where he was going and when he'd be back.

'I thought it would be a bit presumptuous of me to tell you as we'd only just become friendly. I didn't want you to think I was pushing our budding friendship into a personal one.' He paused. 'A romantic one.'

'Well, I'm glad everything is fine, and you're back now.' She kept her tone light, disguising the relief she felt. Seeing him again confirmed something she'd realised last night when she was with Gaven. The laird was handsome, but she wasn't attracted to him in a romantic sense, like she was with Neil.

'Busy morning ahead for you?' he asked.

'Yes, lots of work to do. Sewing, mending, pattern making. Oh and, I have that book of flower photographs to give you. I've sketched everything I need.'

'Are you sure? You're welcome to keep it a while longer.'

'No, I've drawn all the flowers I need. It's right here, on the hall table, so I didn't forget to give it back to you.' She opened her cottage door and stepped inside.

Neil stood outside, peering in, but not overstepping the mark to invite himself inside.

Penny made the offer as she gave him the book. 'Would you like to come in? I was at the bakery for fresh bread and Bradoch's special chocolate loaf.' She held up her bag and then wandered through to the kitchen.

'Chocolate loaf?' He stepped inside and followed her. 'I don't think I've ever had chocolate bread.'

'You don't know what you're missing. Want a cup of tea? I was going to pop the kettle on and then get started on my work.'

'If you're sure I'm not interrupting.'

'Not at all.' Penny put the kettle on to boil, set the cups up and proceeded to cut two slices of the chocolate bread.

Neil looked so tall standing there in her kitchen, filling it with his elegant, broad–shouldered build.

She put the slices on plates and took the butter from the fridge. 'I add a sliver of butter on it.'

'Sounds delicious, and decadent.'

'It is.' She put the plates with the thick–cut chocolate bread and butter on the table.

Neil glanced around. 'This is a pretty kitchen, a pretty cottage.' A pretty owner he thought too, but kept that to himself.

She gestured through to the living room. 'I sew through here, usually at the table near the front window, sometimes by the fire, and I have my sewing machine over here.'

The quick tour ticked all the boxes necessary for Neil to grasp where she worked throughout the day. During the night too. He'd seen her burning the midnight oil on many occasions.

He took particular interest in her fabric stash that was folded on top of a dresser and stacked on a shelf beside the sewing machine.

'My fabric stash is in need of replenishment,' she said. 'It may look like it's trying to overtake everything, but trust me, I go through a lot of fabric for my mending and sewing.'

'That's a relief,' he said, smiling guiltily at her.

Penny frowned. 'What do you mean?'

'I swithered whether to buy piles of fabric pieces that I saw in a shop window in Edinburgh. The colours caught my attention. It was a haberdashery, selling fabric, thread, yarn, and I went in to browse. They were very helpful, especially when I explained what you did for a living.'

Penny wondered if she was hearing right. 'You were browsing in a haberdashery?'

Neil shrugged casually.

The kettle clicked off, interrupting their conversation. Penny hurried through to the kitchen to make the tea.

Neil followed her through. He thumbed behind him. 'There's a...what did you call it? A *fabric stash*? A few fat quarter bundles are in my car. I saw them and thought you might like them.'

Her heart soared. 'You've bought me fabric?'

'If it's of no use to you, I thought I'd give it to the ladies at the crafting bee.' This was his backup plan if Penny wasn't pleased with him for disappearing without a word. And not contacting her when he was in Edinburgh. His reasons for his behaviour were exactly as he'd told her.

Penny stood for a moment before pouring their tea.

'I hope I haven't acted out of turn,' he told her.

'No, why don't you bring them in while I make the tea,' she suggested, hiding how eager she was to see the fabric he'd bought for her.

Neil was back within minutes, his arms filled with a cardboard box brimming with what appeared to be yarn and embroidery thread, and several fat quarter bundles of top quality cotton fabric — solids and patterns, bright colours and pastel tones. The bundles had been selected by the haberdashery and tied with ribbon.

Penny felt the excitement rise in her. 'Put them through in the living room.'

Neil carried them through and put them down on her sewing table.

Penny left their tea and buttered chocolate bread in the kitchen and went through to see the fabric.

The colours looked beautiful. Pale sunlight streamed through the cottage window highlighting the full spectrum of colours. Penny ran her hands over the fabric, itching to organise it and make it part of her fabric stash.

'This is gorgeous!' She loved fabric, and seeing all these wonderful pieces, each one around the size of a pillow case, folded neatly and stacked in attractive bundles tied with ribbons, made her beam with delight.

Neil was relieved. From Penny's reaction, he'd chosen a gift she appreciated.

The quality of the cotton was excellent, and usually she'd wait for bundles like these to be on sale, but she knew Neil had paid full price for them.

'I'm glad you like the fabric.'

'I love it. You know of course that I won't get any work done today because I'll be eyeball deep in sorting through this fabric goldmine.'

He drew her attention to the box of yarn and embroidery thread. 'I'd better put this back in the car then,' he joked.

'Don't you dare!' She delved into the box, lifting out the soft yarn, various colours and textures, plenty of double knit which she used a lot of, and then she gasped when she saw the selection of embroidery thread. 'Did you buy up every colour in the entire range?' The numerous individual skeins of stranded cotton embroidery thread filled the bottom of the box.

'Ah, the embroidery thread was difficult to narrow down. The shop checked out your website and suggested colours to match the solid tones of the fabric, and then other colours that were suitable to blend in with the patterned fabric, the polka dots and floral designs. I didn't know what to choose.'

'So you basically bought them all.'

'Not quite, but almost, nearly. If they're of no use to you I'll—'

Penny cut–in. 'No, these have my name on them now, Neil.' She smiled at him, clearly delighted.

A warmth melted his heart when he looked at her.

Penny took a deep breath. 'Okay, let's get our tea and chocolate bread. Then I'm hustling you out the door, but inviting you to dinner tonight.'

'Dinner? I don't want to put you to any bother.'

She took a sip of her tea. 'It's the least I can do, and I did promise you I'd cook dinner sometime. But...' She sighed. 'Be warned. I may go down the fabric stash rabbit hole and not emerge in time to make dinner. A slice of toast and a run round the kitchen table could be all you get.'

'I'd be fine with that.' Although he was joining in with her light–heartedness, he would be happy just being with her.

He bit into his buttered chocolate bread and nodded, surprised how tasty it was.

'It's scrumptious, isn't it?'

Neil nodded and took another bite.

The ate their bread and drank their tea, content in each other's company.

'Before you hustle me out the door now,' he began, 'is there any gossip that I've missed since I've been away?'

'Tons. A lot of it involving me,' she confessed. 'But most of it isn't true.'

'So some of it is?'

Penny looked guilty. 'It wasn't my fault. Keep that in mind when you hear the scandal.'

'Are you going to tell me?'

'No, I've fabric to stash and work to do. You'll find out when you buy a chocolate loaf at Bradoch's bakery. You intend buying one, don't you?'

'I do. This is on my shopping list now. I didn't even know that chocolate bread was a thing.'

'Well, when you're there, you'll hear the latest gossip involving a haggis going on fire at Gaven's castle...'

Neil's eyebrows raised at the thought of it.

'And a skirmish in the castle's bar restaurant involving Walter. But he was apparently defending my honour after telling the staff that I was canoodling with Gaven.'

'You were kissing Gaven?'

'No, I haven't locked lips with the laird, at all. Nor have I seen his turret.'

Neil laughed. 'This does sound scandalous, and salacious.'

'Entertaining,' Penny corrected him.

'Okay, what else?' he asked her.

She pointed to her ruined beige shoes tucked beside the kitchen sink.

'What happened to your shoes?'

'I did a runner from the castle, at night, through puddles and wet grass. I almost outran Gaven, and he was in his car, but I had a head start.'

'So you can run fast?'

'Very fast, especially when I've been scorched with embarrassment during my tour of the castle. Which was cut short due to the skirmish.'

'For such a sweet natured, innocent looking person, you're a real troublemaker,' he scolded her jokingly.

'Don't say you haven't been warned, Neil.'

'I'll take my chances.'

She smiled, and then looked forlornly at her shoes. She'd tried to wash the grime off, but the pale cream canvas fabric was stained. 'They may be beyond repair, but now that I have lots of fabric to play around with, I'll attempt to cover over the damage.'

Neil downed the last of his tea, smiled, intrigued about the gossip, determined to find out what it was before he came back for dinner.

He headed out, taking the book of flower photographs with him. 'I'll see you tonight then. I'll bring a torch and a hook and line.'

Penny frowned. 'What for?'

'To rescue you out of that rabbit hole if you've gone down too far.'

Penny laughed and waved him off.

Neil started to walk back to his cottage, feeling that the night held the promise of romance and trouble. A potent mix, but he was up for it.

Penny called after him. 'Just one question, Neil.'

He paused, turned, and looked at her.

'When are you going away again without telling me?' she joked with him.

'Never,' he called back to her. 'So you'd better make that fabric last.'

Laughing, she went inside her cottage, looking forward to a fabric–filled day, and dinner that night with Neil.

CHAPTER TEN

Penny mended a few items from her garment rail using colours from the new fabric and embroidery thread. She'd been so busy recently that her fabric stash had become depleted, as had her embroidery thread supply, and she'd intended restocking. So when Neil gave her the surprise gifts, it was very handy.

Her new embroidery patterns, especially the spring flowers — pansy, primrose, snowdrop and crocus designs were starting to sell quite well on her website. She stitched one of the pansies as a pretty motif on to a vintage dress she was mending and then selling. Patchwork repairs to a pair of jeans looked great with some of the new colours of cotton fabric.

She made a start on mending a jumper too, darning the elbows with crewel wool, but stopped as the sky outside the living room window deepened as the day mellowed.

Putting her mending aside, she started to make dinner — Scottish cheddar cheese flan and a tasty selection of vegetables. While the pot of vegetables cooked and the flan was in the oven, Penny tidied herself up and put on a wrap skirt, floral print blouse and a pale pink cardigan. She'd washed her hair that morning so she brushed it straight and silky, and refreshed her makeup, ready for her dinner with Neil.

He arrived on time and knocked on the front door.

'Come in, the door's open,' she called through to him from the kitchen.

She lifted the savoury cheese flan from the oven as he walked in. He looked sharply dressed in a classy shirt, waistcoat and smart trousers. He was carrying a cake box.

'Blame Bradoch,' he said, presenting her with the cake.

She put her oven mitts aside and accepted the box. She peered inside and smiled when she saw a strawberry and berry fruit cream filled sponge cake. Whipped cream was piped around the top and it was decorated with strawberries and brambles.

'You told Bradoch you were having dinner with me?' she said.

'I did. I let slip. I wanted to hear the gossip and couldn't resist buying a cake, my contribution to dinner, which smells delicious.'

Penny put the cake safely aside and started to serve up their meal. 'I hope you like cheese flan and vegetables.'

'I do. Can I help with anything?'

'You could make the tea. The kettle should be boiled in a minute.'

Neil set about making the tea, feeling at home with Penny, while recognising the strong beating of his heart whenever he was near her.

'I rustled up a flan. Someone bought me fabric and thread and the day whizzed by.'

Neil eyed the flan. The Scottish cheddar was melted across the top and decorated with sliced tomatoes. A terrine of hot vegetables sat in the middle of the kitchen table and two place mats that looked liked she'd quilted them herself were set ready for their meal.

She cut two generous slices of the flan and lifted each piece carefully on to their plates.

Neil poured the tea and sat the cups down on the table.

She was relieved that the flan had turned out well. It was one of her go–to recipes.

Sitting down, she scooped two portions of the vegetables on to their plates.

'Help yourself to the condiments,' Penny told him. 'I can recommend the bramble chutney and pickle.'

'I'll try those.' He added them to his plate along with a sprinkling of sea salt on the vegetables.

'Thank you for making dinner, especially as you've had a busy day.'

She smiled across the table at him. 'Did Bradoch update you on the latest gossip?'

Neil grinned and ate a piece of the cheese flan, savouring the lavish topping of Scottish cheddar.

'Did it paint me as a troublemaker?' she asked.

Eating his dinner he nodded.

She viewed him over the rim of her teacup. 'I'm surprised you turned up for dinner, especially with all the canoodling with the laird accusations.'

'I don't believe the gossip. I'm sure there were valid reasons why Gaven was carrying you into the cabin, then doing likewise into his office.'

'It sounds scandalous, but it was entirely innocent.'

'On your part, but perhaps not on Gaven's.'

'Is that what Bradoch told you?'

'Sort of, but it's easy to see that Gaven is interested in you.'

Penny brushed this aside. 'It's because I'm new to the area.'

Neil pressed his lips together.

'What?'

Neil shook his head.

'Come on, out with it,' she insisted.

Neil relaxed back in his chair and gazed over at her. 'It's pretty obvious that Gaven is interested in dating you. I have my reasons for understanding that.'

'What reasons?'

'You're beautiful. Full of energy and fun, talent and kindness. It's a heady mix. Trust me.'

She did trust Neil.

Penny started to blush and focussed on her dinner.

'I'm not trying to embarrass you, Penny.' He took a deep breath. 'I just think that Gaven is accustomed to having women fall for him. You haven't. That makes you different, a challenge. I feel he likes the challenge.'

Penny listened, and ate her dinner, while Neil continued.

'Now I hear he's planning an impromptu ceilidh night at the castle. Bradoch said that Jessy wasn't expecting them to hold another ceilidh party until well into the spring. They think that Gaven is organising it so he can invite you, dance with you and impress his way into your heart.'

'My heart belongs to me,' she said firmly, causing Neil to look slightly crushed. 'Not entirely,' she added quickly. 'I'm taking my time getting to know someone and so far I'm enjoying his company.'

Neil's smile warmed her heart, and for a few moments they sat comfortably enjoying their dinner.

'The thing that concerns me is that a man like Gaven could use his looks, his position as laird, and his castle to change your mind.'

'It won't happen. I'm unbelievably stubborn. It's a trait that I've been told, especially at my previous job, that I need to address. I was described as obstinate and headstrong when it came to my designs. But sometimes being stubborn is an asset.'

'I'd call you persistent when it comes to your work. And tenacious and determined, setting up your business on your own without any outside backing. Your willingness to take a chance is admirable.'

Penny looked at him and smiled.

Neil continued to eat his dinner. 'This cheese flan is so tasty.'

'Any thoughts on what I should do about Gaven?'

'I do, but they could be construed as slanted in my favour,' he told her.

'Tell me.'

He took a deep breath. 'Go with me to the ceilidh party — as my date.' His gorgeous blue eyes glanced over at her, hoping she'd say yes.

'As your date?'

He nodded.

'A proper date?'

'That would be up to you, Penny. But I would hope so. We could still take things slowly. Make the ceilidh our first date. With a get–out clause at the end of the evening. No strings attached, unless you wanted to.'

'This sounds complicated and tricky enough that it could work.' She looked over at him, feeling her heart ache seeing this handsome and intelligent man sitting in her kitchen, offering her a chance for romance.

Neil didn't push her further.

'Okay,' Penny said firmly. 'You've got a date.'

They continued to enjoy their dinner.

'I'd still like to take you on that tour of the area,' he said.

Penny nodded. 'I'm up for that. The weather felt milder this morning. The sun was brighter and there was a definite feeling of spring in the air. If it continues to be nice, we could go sometime during the next few days.'

'We'll do that.'

'But promise you'll warn me if you take me to any other kissing spots. The gossip was rife with that.'

Neil frowned. 'What kissing spot?'

'The one you drove us to in the rain, up on the hill.'

It was Neil's turn to look embarrassed. 'I'd no idea that's what it was.'

'Well, it is. I told Sylvia that nothing like that happened between us. But even Gaven knew about it.'

Neil shook his head, and his embarrassment turned to laughter. 'Of all the places I drove us to...the kissing spot.'

Penny smiled, cleared their plates away and cut two slices of the cake.

Neil topped up their teacups.

'What were your plans for the rest of this evening, before you offered to make dinner?' he said.

'I like to relax in the living room with my sewing. I know it's work, but as I love to sew and find it relaxing, that's what I like to do in the evenings. Often I'll watch a film or television series while I'm working. You're welcome to join me for a little while if you want.'

'Yes, I'd like that. You set up your sewing, find something for us to watch, and I'll make us another round of tea.'

Penny smiled and went through to the lounge. The fire flickered and created a cosiness to the room, as did the glow of the lamps. She set up her sewing as she usually would if she was planning to watch the telly, sitting on the sofa and putting her sewing basket on the table.

She heard Neil making the tea, and for a moment she felt what her life would be like if she was dating him properly, more than friends or a casual relationship. It felt good and her heart was filled with excitement that perhaps this would eventually be true.

'Here we are,' Neil said, bringing their tea through. 'Where should I put it? I don't want to risk spilling it on your sewing. What are you sewing anyway?'

'Appliqué, on a jacket.' She showed him the item with the needleturn appliqué she'd already been working on.

'That looks lovely.' He put her tea down where she could reach it, but away from her sewing.

Then he settled down in one of the chairs beside the fire. 'What are we going to watch?'

'I've been following a spy thriller television series. Would you be up for watching an episode?' She gave him a rundown of the series.

'It sounds great. I've never seen it, but I've heard it's really good.' He relaxed back in his chair, feeling the warmth of the fire, and sipped his tea.

For the next hour, they enjoyed watching television, chatting and relaxing together.

When the episode ended, Neil decided not to outstay his welcome. He got up to leave.

'I'm going to let you get on with your sewing,' he said. 'Thank you again for dinner and a lovely evening.'

The piles of fabric he'd gifted to her were now part of her stash, along with the thread and the yarn. Penny motioned towards them. 'I appreciate all the things you bought for me, Neil. It was very thoughtful of you.'

Neil smiled and bid her goodnight. 'Don't get up. I'll see myself out.'

She heard the door close as he left, and something deep inside her longed for him to stay. She shook the feeling off and concentrated on her sewing, then continued watching the next episode while sewing late into the night.

There was Penny's cottage, lit up in the darkness. Gaven hadn't seen her since she'd run away from the castle. He hoped she'd go to the ceilidh party he was planning. He was looking forward to dancing with her.

Gaven ran along the edge of the loch, powering through the late evening air, feeling the brisk energy as he increased his pace, and raced back up to the castle.

The scent of the fresh flowers on display outside the flower shop wafted in the air. Penny walked along the main street having dropped more parcel orders off at the post office, topped up on a few groceries, and now headed home, taking the route that let her have a look at the flower shop.

The afternoon sunlight shone in the pale blue sky, and reflected off the front window of the shop. The day had been mild, again hinting that spring was on its way.

The array of flowers, from tulips to little bouquets of spring blossoms hand tied with pretty twine, enticed Penny to gaze at the lovely colours. A small bunch of mixed flowers, with colours ranging from primrose yellow to lilac, warm pinks and fresh green, looked beautiful.

The exterior of the shop was painted cream and the large window displayed other items for sale including fluted glass vases, ornamental baskets, ceramic flower pots and window box containers.

Penny was so busy admiring the flowers that she blinked when the owner, a tall, lean, man in his early thirties, stepped outside the doorway. His thick blonde hair had an unruly look to it and his light blue eyes were a fair match for the open neck shirt he was wearing, along with a pair of jeans and sturdy boots. He wore a florist's apron made from quality linen, and his hands were pushed into the apron's pockets.

'Can I help you?' he said in a voice that had a deep resonance.

This must be Fyn, the owner, Penny thought, having heard Etta and the other ladies describe the handsome florist.

Maybe it was the spring sunlight that highlighted his tall stature and manly presence, but the description she'd heard from them was merited. Fyn was a real looker with a sexy but welcoming smile.

'I'd like to buy one of the little bunches of mixed spring flowers,' she told him, pointing to the ones she wanted.

Fyn stepped beside her, and she estimated that he was probably as tall as Neil.

'These ones?' He lifted the bunch she seemed interested in and gently shook the water from the stems where it had been sitting in the display container.

'Yes, I'll take those.'

Fyn smiled and took the flowers inside the shop.

Penny followed him, admiring the light cream decor of the interior. Shelves were adorned with decorative flower pots in pastel blues, pinks and greens, and he sold floral cards and wrapping paper. Coloured glass vases caught the sunlight as did the ribbons on the rail behind the counter.

Without asking, Fyn pulled a length of turquoise blue ribbon and tied it around the bunch of flowers. They were already secured with twine, but this was something he added for each purchase.

Penny got ready to pay for the flowers, but was taken aback when he wrapped the flowers in floral print paper and handed them to her, saying, 'There you go, Penny.'

Her reaction made him explain. 'The crafting bee ladies told me.'

'They told me you were Fyn.' They'd also emphasised during the chatter at the recent bee night, how gorgeous he was, but she kept that snippet to herself.

She paid for the flowers, loving the scent of them. She planned to put them in her kitchen, sketch some of them, but mainly enjoy a bunch of fresh spring flowers in her cottage.

'Would you like some flower scatter?' he said, gesturing through to the back of his shop where he cut and trimmed the flowers.

Penny frowned. 'Flower scatter?'

'Wee bits and pieces that aren't fit for sale. Flower heads or those with stems that are too short to make a bouquet. Trimmings from the greenery, fronds, leaves, that sort of thing.' He headed through to the back of the shop. 'Come through, I'll show you.' He beckoned her to go with him.

Penny followed him through to where his workshop was tucked out of view. It smelled of fresh greenery, gardenia and freesia. The premises looked like a converted cottage, and this was the original kitchen area. The back door was open and she could see a garden and a shed outside.

Packets of flower seeds were stacked up on a sturdy wooden table in his workshop, and it looked like he'd been filling these for sale.

Fyn showed her a handful of flower scatter beside the large sink where he'd been cutting and trimming flowers.

'A few of the crafting bee ladies find the scatter useful,' he said. 'They press the flower heads, use them for sketching designs, like yourself and Robin, all sorts of crafts and uses. I don't like waste and it's a pity to throw them away, so I offer them to customers.'

'Yes, I'll take some,' Penny said, getting ready to pay for them.

Fyn shook his head. 'There's no charge. I give these away. As I say, I'd throw them away in any case.' He lifted a couple of handfuls, put them on a sheet of white wrapping paper, folded them expertly into an envelope shape and stuck on a little label with his shop's logo to secure it.

He handed the flower and greenery filled envelope to Penny. 'There you go.'

'Thank you, that's very kind.'

'Everyone around here tries to help each other. Speaking of which...Oliver showed me the apron you mended for him.'

Penny looked surprised. 'He did?'

'He came in to show it off. I loved the look you'd given his apron. It's ideal for promoting his business. So I was hoping you'd do the same for me. A different design on my florist's aprons of course.'

He unhooked two clean aprons from a cupboard near the kitchen door. They were pale blue linen–cotton, quite a heavyweight fabric, with a bib and broad straps that crossed over his back and shoulders.

'I have my aprons made by a couple of the bee ladies.' He handed them to Penny.

'This is excellent quality fabric. You'll get a lot of wear from these. The pockets are double–stitched for extra strength.' The aprons weren't as long as Oliver's and the straps were broader. She started to picture adding patchwork and maybe appliqué to them.

'I know nothing about sewing,' he told her. 'Would you need to make different pockets, like you did for Oliver, or sew patchwork pieces on them?'

'I could do either, or both, depending on what you'd prefer.'

Fyn shrugged. 'I don't know what I'd prefer, so maybe I could let you do your creative mending and redesigning. I'm sure you'll make a good job of it. And I'm like Oliver. I love plenty of colour. I'm planning to have photos taken wearing the new style aprons for my website.'

Penny smiled to herself. He'd definitely been chatting to Oliver, but they seemed to be friends, rather than rivals.

She folded the aprons and tucked them in her bag. 'I'll take them with me and bring them back when they're done.'

'Brilliant. Would you be able to add a bit of colour to the straps?'

'Yes, I'll do that.' The ideas were already starting to form in her mind. They were nice aprons, and with the new fabric she had to select from, she imagined how great they could look.

Penny left the flower shop, planning to work on them that evening.

CHAPTER ELEVEN

Penny walked past Neil's cottage on her way to a crafting evening at Etta's cottage. The lights shone from inside, and she smiled to herself, knowing he'd be busy in his workshop. They'd both been busy, but she was looking forward to a day out with him soon, touring the area.

Tonight, she'd been invited to join a crafting evening at Etta's, and had packed one of Fyn's aprons in her craft bag, along with thread and pieces of fabric she intended using to upgrade the apron. She'd also filled a bag with spare bits of fabric from the bundles Neil had given her and a few skeins of embroidery thread to share with the ladies.

Etta's cottage wasn't far, and she saw a couple of ladies heading inside. It was a traditional white cottage with a lovely garden. The front door was open and she stepped inside, feeling the warmth and hearing the laughter, chatter and rattle of teacups as the ladies helped to set things up. The aroma of home baking indicated there were tasty cakes and scones to accompany the tea.

Etta smiled when she saw Penny. 'I'm glad you could come. Make yourself at home.'

Penny took her jacket off, hung it in the hall and joined the hub in the living room. The decor was homely, long–established comfort, with a fire burning in the hearth.

Aileen, Robin and Sylvia where there along with several other ladies. They were seated on the couch and folding chairs. The crafting bee members often held extra get together evenings in their houses as well as attending the weekly night at the castle.

Etta had a cutting table set up along with a sewing machine near her stash of yarn. It was a substantial stash. There was no doubt that knitting was Etta's main craft, but she was a keen quilter too. Quilting seemed to be one of the main things the ladies were working on — fussy cutting fabric, English paper piecing and sewing hexies for quilts and quilted items.

Aileen was helping Robin cut wadding and backing fabric for the quilted piece of textile art, a wall quilt, Robin was making.

Penny sat down on one of the chairs and put the bag of fabric and thread on a table. 'I brought some spare bits and pieces. Help yourselves.'

Etta carried a tray of hot buttered fruit scones and cupcakes through to the living room. 'That's very kind of you, Penny.'

Sylvia followed Etta, carrying a tea tray, and put it down. Sylvia had arrived early to discuss Oliver with Etta. She confided to Etta that she felt miffed that Oliver didn't want her in his painting. But after talking it through with Etta, she agreed that if only one person was in each shop painting, she was happy that it was her Aunt Muira.

The ladies were very interested in Penny's fabric and thread, and she explained about Neil's gift to her.

'You seem to be getting along well with Neil,' said Etta.

Penny nodded. 'We are, but we're taking things slowly, getting to know each other.'

Jessy was hand stitching a quilt using a variegated cotton thread in shades of pink. 'Gaven has arranged for the ceilidh night next weekend. The function room won't be available for our bee night, but we sometimes have to skip one evening for the party nights.'

'We'll have an extra night here,' Etta told them. 'We won't miss out.'

'Are you going to the ceilidh with Neil?' Sylvia asked Penny.

'Yes, he's asked me to go with him,' Penny told her.

Etta offered Penny a buttered scone. 'As his date?'

Penny accepted a scone and nodded.

'Oooh!' Sylvia said, giggling. 'Gaven won't be thrilled about that.'

'I'm really not interested in getting involved with Gaven,' Penny explained. 'When I'm with him I don't feel...'

Jessy spoke up. 'You don't get the vapours.'

Penny blushed and the ladies laughed.

'No, I don't,' Penny said, smiling.

'But you do when you're with Neil?' Etta prompted Penny.

Penny laughed, and then took a bite of her hot buttered scone as the chatter and gossip circled around her.

They spoke about Oliver being delighted with his apron, and Penny told them that she'd met Fyn and he wanted her to embellish his aprons.

Penny showed them the apron she'd brought. 'I've got a piece of cotton–linen fabric that has a Scottish thistle print. I thought I'd use that on the pockets.' She showed them the thistle fabric.

'I love that fabric,' Aileen said, coming over to have a look at it. 'I'd like to stock that in my quilt shop. I like that the thistles are quite big. A bold design like that would look wonderful on a quilt.'

'It was in my stash. I thought the lilac, purple and green tones would look great with the pale blue of the apron.' Penny held them up to show them how well the colours worked.

'It's a good quality fabric,' Aileen remarked.

'I'll give you a link to where I bought it,' Penny said to Aileen.

'Thanks. Floral prints are my top selling quilting fabrics, and those thistles are quite dynamic,' said Aileen.

'Fyn wants me to add whatever I want,' Penny explained. 'I've got a pattern I've used a few times for a thistle appliqué. I thought I'd stitch that on to the apron, and add colourful details to the straps.'

'You're welcome to use my sewing machine tonight,' Etta told Penny.

'Thanks, Etta, I'll do that,' said Penny.

'What did you think of Fyn?' Sylvia said to Penny. 'Gorgeous, isn't he?'

'Oh, yes,' Penny agreed.

'Fyn's a local lad,' said Etta. 'His family owns one of the farms near here. His brother, another looker, still works on the farm, but Fyn opened the flower shop when the premises became available. The previous owner, a gardener, retired.'

'I saw that there's a garden and shed at the back of the shop,' said Penny.

Sylvia grinned. 'So Fyn invited you through the back, eh?'

'He was offering me some flower scatter,' Penny explained. 'I'd bought a wee bunch of spring flowers. He says he gives it to his customers rather than throw it away.'

'He does,' said Robin. 'Every time I buy flowers from him, he gives me extra scatter. I like Fyn.'

Robin's remarked sparked the ladies interest.

'Does Fyn give you the vapours?' Jessy said to Robin, jokingly.

'No, well, no...' Robin said, sounding unsure.

The ladies giggled.

'Fyn's single. He's not dating anyone at the moment,' Jessy told Robin. 'Maybe he'll ask you to dance with him at the ceilidh.'

'Maybe, but the ceilidh nights are lively,' said Robin. 'We all end up dancing with most of the men during the reels.'

'Oliver is single too,' said Etta. 'If it's true that he's secretly in love with one of the local ladies, we could find out which one.'

'It's not me,' Aileen emphasised.

Penny knew from Oliver that she was right. It wasn't Aileen he was in love with. And she didn't think it was Sylvia either. Perhaps it was Robin, she surmised, but kept this thought to herself.

As the evening wore on, more tea, scones and cake was consumed, along with shared skills.

Penny used Etta's sewing machine to stitch the fabric embellishments on to the straps of Fyn's apron. Some of the ladies came over to see her methods.

'I'll sew the thistle patches on to the pockets by hand,' Penny explained as she machined part of the apron.

'That looks lovely,' Jessy remarked. 'You're a fast worker.'

'I've been sewing since I was a wee girl,' Penny explained. 'This is the type of work I've been doing for years. I really enjoy it. Even when I look busy, I actually find it relaxing.'

'I love slow stitching the binding on to a quilt,' Jessy told her.

'I always look forward to settling down with my knitting and watching something on the telly,' Etta chipped–in.

The others agreed.

Penny told them about watching the television series with Neil.

'It sounds as if he's quite at home with you,' Jessy said to Penny.

Penny nodded thoughtfully. A sense of longing took her by surprise. Was she really going to settle down with Neil?

'Gaven would do well to settle down or relax more,' Jessy remarked. 'Those late night runs along the loch must be exhausting after he's been up early and working all day.'

'He'll settle down when he meets the right woman,' said Etta. 'He just hasn't found her yet.'

'Gaven's away on a lot of business trips too,' Sylvia added. 'And when he's at the castle, he's always on hand to deal with running that.'

'Perhaps Gaven doesn't need to change. Maybe he just needs to find a woman tuned in to the same high frequency as him,' Penny suggested.

The ladies considered this.

Etta nodded. 'You're a bundle of energy, Penny. Maybe that's why Gaven's so taken with you.'

'Gaven's mentioned to me about you sewing late into the night,' Jessy told Penny. 'He sounded intrigued and impressed rather than concerned that you were too much of a livewire for his tastes.'

'That's the solution if you want to put Gaven off from fancying you,' Sylvia said light–heartedly to Penny. 'Sleep in during the mornings. Lounge around all day in your pyjamas and watch endless episodes of your favourite television series while munching sweeties. Preferably bought from my sweet shop,' she added with a grin.

Penny laughed. 'Don't tempt me. There are parts of your suggestion that sound enticing.'

One of the ladies joined in, jokingly. 'I do that sometimes anyway. Now I know why Gaven has never invited me on a romantic tour of his castle and turret.'

The ladies laughed.

During the evening, Penny worked on Fyn's apron, almost finishing it, except for the thistle appliqué. She joined in the gossip, exchanged more sewing tips, and wondered what to wear to the ceilidh.

'Guests are requested to wear something appropriate,' Jessy advised Penny. 'It doesn't have to be a special outfit, and men aren't required to wear kilts, though most do, including Gaven.'

'I have a black velvet, tartan backed waistcoat I made for a New Year ceilidh in Glasgow a couple of years ago.' Penny remembered that she liked it, but hadn't worn it since. It had to be tucked away in her wardrobe. 'I could wear it with a white blouse, a black wrap skirt and black pumps.'

'That sounds perfect,' Jessy told Penny.

Penny wondered if Neil would wear a kilt, and the thought of this sent a rush of excitement through her.

'I do love a man in a kilt,' Robin remarked. 'I've been to a few ceilidh nights, and enjoyed them. But I'm not too confident that I know all the dances.'

Jessy brushed Robin's concern aside. 'You'll get whirled around in the energy and excitement of it.'

Etta giggled. 'Remember the night Gaven's kilt whirled a wee bit too high?'

Jessy scolded her playfully. 'Don't even mention that to Gaven. He didn't intend giving the guests an eyeful of his particulars.'

Penny's eyes widened. 'Do the men really go commando under their kilts?'

'Och, yes!' said Jessy. 'But that's part of the fun, and tradition.'

Penny felt herself react to the thought of Neil being the traditional type.

'I expect Neil to wear a kilt, though he may opt for trews,' Jessy told Penny. 'He turned up to one of the Christmas parties, but the men wore suits for that. At New Year he said he was busy working. He's often a very busy man.'

'I like when they wear trews and those lace up ghillie shirts,' said Aileen. 'It's such a manly and romantic look.'

The ladies agreed.

'Do you have a hot date for the ceilidh?' Jessy asked Aileen.

Aileen scoffed. 'Chance would be a fine thing.'

'Neither do I,' Sylvia said, sighing with disappointment.

'We'll do what we usually do,' said Etta. 'We'll go as a wee group, like a girls' night out, and see where the evening takes us.'

This plan was agreed, and apart from a couple of the ladies attending the ceilidh with their husbands, the other bee members were meeting up to arrive together.

As the evening at Etta's cottage came to a close, the ladies filtered out into the night. Robin promised to hold a textile art craft evening at her cottage soon, and one of the other ladies said she would arrange a jewellery making get together at her house.

Penny wondered if she could hold a creative mending night at her cottage. She'd need a few folding chairs, but this was something she hoped to do as she'd enjoyed her extra evening of crafting with the ladies.

Walking past Neil's cottage, Penny noticed that the lights were still on. She was tempted to drop by, discuss the ceilidh, but instead she kept on walking back home. She'd talk to him in the morning. They'd agreed that if the weather was fair, they'd go for their tour of the area.

Penny lit the fire in the living room, having no intention of being sensible and having an early night. Besides, she wanted to check if she had the velvet and tartan waistcoat.

While the fire crackled, building up warmth, and the kettle boiled for tea, she rummaged in the depths of her wardrobe and gave a triumphant smile when she found the waistcoat carefully folded in the depths of it. She'd had the sense to fold it neatly and put it in a bag, so it was in pristine condition. Her white blouse was hanging up, and her wrap skirt hung over the bar of a coat hanger. A quick iron and they'd be ready for the ceilidh. She had two pairs of black pumps, and so she was set for a night of lively dancing.

While she was in the bedroom, she changed out of her clothes and into a pair of cosy jim–jams. Her usual pairs were in the wash, and she wore the bunny print ones that were extra snuggly. She'd bought them as a bargain because they were so cute and cosy, but as she wasn't dating anyone, no one had seen her in them, and she'd no intention of letting anyone do so. She wore them with colourful knitted socks and fluffy slippers.

Making a cup of tea, she took it through to the living room, unpacked her craft bag and hung Fyn's apron on her garment rail. Instead of working on it, or other mending, she opened her laptop and searched for videos showing ceilidh dancing to brush up on her steps. The turns were the things that confused her the most, and she didn't want to ruin a reel by dancing the wrong way.

Taking a slurp of tea, she kicked her slippers off and cleared a space in the middle of the living room to practice the dances in time to the videos.

At the third attempt she got the turns right on one dance.

'One down, lots to go,' she told herself, determined to brush up on her moves. It was late, but then her nights were always busy, and at least this incorporated exercise. By the time she was finished she pictured she'd flop into bed, conk out like a light and sleep sound until the morning.

That was her plan.

Neil had caught a glimpse of Penny walking past his cottage heading home. He finished tidying up the jewellery he'd been working on, and checked the weather forecast. His heart sank when he saw that rain was in the offing. The day out with Penny would have to be postponed. He decided to pop over to her cottage to tell her. He was sure he wouldn't disturb the night owl he knew he was falling for.

As he approached Penny's cottage, he saw that her living room lights were on. He thought she'd be sewing, doing her mending, relaxing by the fire.

But as he glanced in the window, he saw her wearing cute pyjamas — and she was dancing around in her living room like a bunny possessed.

He paused and watched her antics, smiling to himself, adoring her even more.

Should he disturb her? Or pretend he hadn't noticed her wild dancing. It was like watching a fluffy pink and white bunny dancing the Highland fling.

That's when it dawned on him. She was practising the dances for the ceilidh. Something he should do, but over the years he'd attended plenty of them and was confident he could handle the reels and jigs. He owned a kilt, a full Highland outfit, so he was kitted out for the ceilidh. He smiled again, watching Penny dancing, and then decided to knock on her door, let her know he'd seen her rather than be sneaky.

The knock on the door jarred Penny. She checked the time. Why was someone at her door at this time of night?

She padded in her socks over to the window and peered out.

Neil smiled and waved in, trying to look casual.

Penny hurried through and opened the door.

'Sorry to disturb your...dancing,' he apologised.

She cringed from head to mended socks toes.

'Don't be embarrassed. I assume you're practising for the ceilidh.'

'Yes.' She smiled, trying not to squirm that he'd seen her.

'I couldn't help but notice as I went by the window,' he explained.

'It's fine,' she lied. 'Is there something wrong?'

'The weather forecast for the next few days is rain, a bit overcast. So I thought we should postpone our day out touring until the weather is brighter. You'll get the benefit of the views better.'

'Yes, let's do that. We could go after the ceilidh night,' she suggested.

Neil agreed. He was standing outside the cottage, and she suddenly realised she should invite him in.

The evening was quite cold, and he wore an open neck shirt, without a jumper or jacket.

'Come in out of the cold.' She invited him in, feeling that rush of excitement whenever she was near him.

Neil stepped inside. 'I won't stay long. I don't want to interrupt your dance practice.'

She led him through to the living room and showed him the dance she was trying to learn. 'The turns are what I usually get wrong. I go right when I should go left.' She ran her hands through her silky blonde hair, causing Neil to be distracted by her loveliness.

He glanced at her bunny outfit, but made no comment.

She caught the look. 'My other jim–jams are in the wash. I didn't expect to have company.'

'They look comfy,' he said, trying to sound as if his heart wasn't melting just looking at her. Even when wearing an outfit like this, Penny was capable of stealing his heart.

'I found these dance videos. From ceilidh nights I've been to, I remember these were popular.' She played the video she was watching. 'This dance, one of the reels, is fast–moving, so I'm trying to learn it so I don't faff it up at the castle.'

'I know this one.' He held out his hands. 'Do you want to try it with a partner?'

'Eh, yes.' She took his hands and they started to dance around, with Neil keeping her right when she had a tendency to go left.

'Keep going, Penny. Even if you get it wrong, keep dancing, don't stop. That causes more chaos.'

'Okay,' she said, crossing her hands over and grasping hold of Neil's hands as he burled her around the living room.

As they continued he started laughing.

'What are you laughing at? I'm trying my best.'

'At us. Look at us. Two crazy night owls in the Scottish Highlands. One dressed as a bunny.'

Penny laughed too. 'I did warn you, Neil. I'm nothing but trouble. You'd be doing the sensible thing. You'd have finished work, and gone to bed at a decent time.'

'I'm impressed,' he said.

'By what? My dancing is subpar.'

He shook his head. 'At your fitness. You can talk while you're wild dancing.'

Penny smiled. 'So can you, Neil.'

'Perhaps we're even better suited than we thought.'

Penny nodded, and then let him lead her around the floor, whirling to the sounds of the Scottish music.

After several dances, Penny flopped down on the sofa. 'I'm puggled.'

Neil sat down beside her. 'You've worn me out too.'

Penny giggled. 'It takes a brave man to admit that.'

He gave her a scolding look. 'You know what I mean.'

She did, but enjoyed teasing him.

Neil sank back on the sofa. 'Wake me when it's morning.' He checked the time on his wristwatch. 'Which should be in the next ten minutes.'

Penny scolded him lightly. 'It's only just past the Cinderella hour.'

Neil raised his eyebrows, disagreeing.

'Okay, so an hour later than that. But time flies when you're having fun.'

'It was fun. Exhausting. Not what I planned after a full day's work.'

Penny sighed and nodded. 'We should both be tucked up in bed.'

Neil glanced at her and smiled.

'What I mean is, in bed in our cottages,' she quickly corrected herself. 'Not snuggled up in bed together.'

Neil continued to smile as Penny dug herself deeper with her comments.

'You know fine what I mean, Neil.'

'Unfortunately, I do.' He pushed himself reluctantly up from the sofa. 'Okay, I'll let you get some sleep.' He headed though to the hall and opened the front door.

'I have a lot of work, sewing and patterns to design,' she said. 'So let's agree to meet up for the ceilidh, and in the meantime, get on with our businesses.'

Neil nodded. 'I'm looking forward to going to the castle with you.'

Bidding each other goodnight, Neil walked home to his cottage, and Penny started to get ready for bed.

Lying under the covers, gazing out at the night sky, she pictured what it would be like if Neil was there with her, snuggling close.

And with thoughts of Neil and the ceilidh at the castle, she fell sound asleep.

CHAPTER TWELVE

The rain gave a cosiness to the day, blanketing out the world, casting the surrounding hills in a fine mist, as Penny worked on her sewing inside her cottage.

The warmth from the fire made the living room a comforting niche where she could cut pieces of fabric for the appliqué thistle for Fyn's apron, and then create a flower garden and heather design for his other apron.

The sound of the rain on the windows added to the cosy feeling, as she sat snug and safe in her cottage.

She'd chopped fresh vegetables after breakfast — carrots, onions, white cabbage, turnip and leek, and a pot of lentil and vegetable soup was now cooking in the kitchen. The tasty aroma added to the homely atmosphere.

The needleturn appliqué had a calming effect. She turned in the edges of the fabric with her needle as she stitched it. This created a neat edging to the designs and it looked effective when she'd finished them.

The porridge she'd had for breakfast kept her going until lunch. She put her sewing aside and sat down in the kitchen to enjoy a hearty bowl of soup and bread. The rain created a soft focus view of her back garden and hills beyond.

The spring flowers she'd bought sat in a glass vase at the kitchen window and the light fragrance was lovely. The scatter Fyn had given her had been put to use. She'd arranged the flower heads and leaves on a sheet of white paper, dotting them around as if they were a fabric print. Then she took photographs of it with the purpose of creating an embroidery pattern suitable for border designs.

Penny couldn't bring herself to bin the pretty flower heads, so she pressed them between the pages of an old paperback book and weighted it down.

She loved pressed flowers and they reminded her of times past when she'd pick flowers as a child and then tuck them into the pages of her favourite story books. Often, the books went adrift as she travelled onwards with her parents, but she liked the whole aspect of flower pressing. She could make something that would fade and wither, long–lasting. Maybe now that she was settled in her cottage, she'd come across the pressed flower book a season or two down the line, and make the flowers into a piece of artwork for her wall.

After lunch, she continued sewing, and packed the orders for items customers had purchased from her website.

Later, while she had the iron out pressing Fyn's finished aprons, she ran it over her blouse and skirt for the ceilidh. It would be one less task to do on the night of the party when she'd no doubt be in a tizzy getting ready for her date with Neil.

She ironed her outfit and then hung it up in the wardrobe.

From the depths of the wardrobe, she dug out her red wool coat. She'd bought it for a bargain price online. The quality was excellent and the only thing that was wrong with it was the torn lining. Snapping up the bargain buy, she'd repaired the silky red lining, mending it, making the barely worn coat as good as new again. No one was going to inspect the lining, and even if they did, she'd made a feature of the rip, embroidering it with a trailing stitch stem with climbing roses. The coat was warm and perfect for her night out. She always felt dressy and classy when she wore it.

For her afternoon tea break, she put aside the motifs she was embroidering on a jacket, made a cuppa and cut a slice of Scottish fruit loaf. By the time she'd finished this, the rain had eased to a fine drizzle, so she decided to take her parcels earlier than planned to the post office.

She tucked her slim–fitting dark cords into her waterproof walking boots and put on her hooded raincoat. The three–quarter length coat with its floral print was another pre–loved buy. The toggles were the only repair needed. Some were missing or dangling, so she'd replaced them with a new set. Apart from that, the coat was a handy and fashionable addition to her wardrobe, and certainly useful for rainy days in Scotland.

With her hood up, and carrying her parcels and Fyn's aprons in a bag, she ventured out into the smirry rain. It fell in a blanket of mist with barely a breeze, so it felt like walking through a hazy watercolour day. The scent of the greenery, the heather and the early spring flowers created an invigorating atmosphere. She almost wished the few minutes walk to the post office was longer.

After dropping the parcels off, she headed to Fyn's flower shop.

She walked in and wondered where he was. There were no customers, only her, though wet footprints led through to the back of the shop and she followed them to find Fyn outside in his garden. The shed door was open and it looked like he'd been working in the rain. His blond hair was damp, as were the shoulders of his denim shirt.

'Fyn,' she called out to him.

He looked round and smiled, then strode towards her carrying a flower pot and trowel.

'Sorry, I've been potting plants.'

She held up his aprons, neatly folded. 'I'll leave these out of dripping distance.' She glanced at the raindrops on the tips of his hair.

He put the pot and trowel down, and ran his hands through his thick, wet hair, sweeping it back from his sculptured features.

'I can't wait to see what you've done with them.' He quickly rinsed his hands in the sink, dried them and lifted the top apron.

He looked delighted when he saw the thistle design she'd added to it.

'Avert your eyes,' he told her.

She frowned, then immediately looked away as he took his wet shirt off and shrugged on a clean one that was hanging in the kitchen area cupboard.

Shame on her, she had a peek, and then blushed seeing his buff body.

'You're peeking, Penny.'

'I'm not,' she lied, blushing.

He smiled and couldn't wait to try the apron on. He didn't have a mirror, so he used his reflection in the window to view it.

'The design works.' Penny sounded relieved.

'It's great,' he told her, resisting giving her a hug of thanks for the obvious trouble she'd gone to. She'd made it extra special. He'd seen how much she charged for her work on her website. He was happy to pay and intended giving her a bonus.

'Want to try the other one on?' She held it up, again taking him by surprise.

He'd assumed she'd be using the same design or a similar one on the second apron. But no. Penny had outdone herself again.

'A flower garden!' he exclaimed, loving the way she'd sewn the colourful flowers along the bottom of the apron, and accented it with sunflowers, chocolate cosmos and leaves on the pockets. 'This is incredible.'

'The aprons should look good on your website.'

'They're just what I need to promote my shop,' he said. 'While you're here, would you mind taking some pictures?'

She smiled and accepted his phone to snap the photos. 'Stand through in the front shop. The light is better there.'

He did as she suggested and stood beside the window wearing the flower garden apron.

'Okay, these look good. Put the thistle apron on now and stand over near the counter,' she instructed him.

'You're used to doing this, aren't you?' he said, posing wherever Penny placed him, smiling, holding up a bunch of flowers, whatever she had in mind.

'It was part of my previous job to organise aspects of the fashion and design shoots,' she told him.

'Do you miss it? The city? Or will you settle here in the village?'

'I'm definitely staying. I don't miss the city. I spent years travelling the world, only to fortunately find everything I need and love here.'

'You can have a big life in a small world,' Fyn told her thoughtfully. 'And vice versa.'

Penny nodded firmly. 'That's true.'

She finished taking the photos and handed his phone back to him. He flicked through the pictures, nodding and thanking her.

'Are you looking forward to the ceilidh at the castle?' he said.

'Yes, Neil's taking me.'

'I heard. Bradoch is a worse gossip than Etta,' he joked. 'Everyone I know is going, so I'll see you there. The ceilidh nights are wonderful.'

'I've heard they're wild too.'

'Very, so wear your dancing shoes and be prepared for a real Highland fling.'

'I'm all set.'

Penny waved to Fyn as she left, and then popped into the bakery for a fresh loaf and was tempted to buy an apple pie.

'What's your secret?' Penny said to Bradoch as she paid for the items.

Bradoch frowned.

'I only came in for a loaf, as I always do, and each time I leave with scones, a cake, chocolate bread, or...an apple pie.'

Bradoch laughed. 'It's the tasty aroma of the baking. It lures the unwary to succumb to the other treats on offer.'

'It certainly works,' she said, smiling, and then headed out.

Smirry rain cast the main street in a pale grey haze and the late afternoon was edging into early evening. She pulled up the hood of her coat and breathed in the fresh air. She loved sunny days, but there was something wonderful about walking in the rain when she was dressed for the weather.

Heading home, she saw the loch in the distance. There was no reflection on it, only the ripples caused by the rain. The white cottages dotted around the loch and hills stood out in the magnificent grey haze. None had yet turned their lights on. She'd never seen the landscape look like this, so innately Scottish and deeply beautiful.

The handful of days until the ceilidh night, flew by. Penny had brief moments with Neil. They'd waved to each other and he'd called her to arrange when to pick her up for the party.

Apart from that, she'd concentrated on her work, and tucked herself into the cottage on the rainy days leading up to the event at the castle.

Nervous excitement charged through her as she stood in front of the wardrobe mirror wearing her outfit for the ceilidh.

She wore her hair down and played up her grey eyes with silver grey eye shadow and mascara.

Smoothing down her skirt, she checked that her waistcoat fitted well over her white blouse. She put her shoes on and picked up her clutch bag. She was ready to go.

Neil knocked on the front door, arriving on time.

She hurried through to the hall.

Her heart thundered in anticipation regarding what he'd be wearing as she opened the door.

But nothing could've prepared her for the effect he had on her when she saw him standing there in his kilt. He was the most handsome kiltie she'd ever seen.

Neil smiled at her. 'You look beautiful, Penny.'

She was sure she swooned just looking at him and seeing him smiling at her. And she was pretty sure she'd never swooned before.

'Are you okay?' Those stunning blue eyes of his showed his concern.

'Yes, fine, totally okay, ready to go, I'm up for it,' she said in one hurried sentence.

Neil didn't question her, but clearly she wasn't okay.

His car was parked outside. He'd no intention of walking to the castle, especially as it could rain. But the day had been a bright one, and he was hopeful he'd be able to take Penny on that tour soon.

Penny stepped outside, forgetting her coat, too excited about the whole event. She'd been thinking about it all day, and the previous day. Now that Neil was there and they were about to set off, the fireworks of excitement ignited inside her, causing her to forget that she wanted to wear it.

Neil saw the red coat hanging in the hall. He hadn't seen her red wool coat before and rightly assumed she intended wearing it that evening.

'You forgot your coat,' he said.

'Oh, yes.' She stepped back in, unhooked it and shrugged it on. 'I'm a bit wound up.'

'Anything wrong? Something that's knocked you off kilter?' Neil asked, escorting her to his car.

'Just excitement. Hoping I don't mess up the dances,' she told him. It was part truth, edged with lies. The truth was, seeing Neil dressed like he belonged on the cover of a hot romance novel, threw her for a loop. Not that she was complaining. She'd expected he'd be well–dressed and wearing a kilt. But seeing him, tall, broad shouldered, with a lace up ghillie shirt just waiting for her fingers to unravel it rattled her resolve to be calm. He wore a cropped jacket, unbuttoned, that exposed the shirt front and emphasised his broad shoulders.

Shame on her for thinking thoughts that disturbed her senses. And of course there was the issue of — was Neil going commando under his kilt?

Do. Not. Think. This. She scolded herself as Neil helped her into the passenger seat, unaware of the scorching flashes of unwanted and slightly scandalous thoughts whirring through her mind.

As Neil started up the car and drove them off, heading towards the castle, she realised that above all else, she'd missed him. She'd missed Neil in the past few days. The momentary exchanges were too fleeting, but she'd certainly got a lot of work done. But that was the only bonus.

Now here she was, heading for a romantic night at the castle. Their first date.

Did that make her Neil's girlfriend? She wasn't sure of the rules of romance. She'd been out of the game, or playing around on the edges of it, for too long. She needed an update on where she stood with him.

'You're very quiet,' he said gently, hoping he hadn't overdone the ghillie shirt, kilt and sporran attire. Maybe Penny preferred him in a suit.

She smiled tightly, pressing her lips together so she didn't say anything awkward until she'd calmed down a bit. Perhaps that was what exacerbated her feelings. She'd been out in the romantic wilderness for too long.

She breathed deeply. Or maybe there was an easier explanation. Neil was sexy, handsome and luscious. In that order, or any order. And she was in danger of falling hard for the gorgeous goldsmith.

'I don't usually wear a kilt,' he began to apologise, deciding he was the cause of her lack of cheery chatter.

Neil was right, she thought. But he was also entirely wrong.

'I love your kilt. You really suit it,' she said, hoping he didn't hear the nervous tone in her voice.

He felt better, but wondered if the shirt was the problem.

As far as Penny was concerned, that shirt was a problem she loved having.

'The ghillie shirt is an acquired taste,' he said. 'For other functions, like weddings, I wear a buttoned shirt, tie, waistcoat and jacket. But it's bound to get hot during the ceilidh dancing, so I wore this.'

'Great idea. You suit that shirt.'

By now, they were driving up to the castle. The beautiful architecture looked impressive against the dark, night sky.

Neil drove them through the ornate entrance leading up to the castle. The windows were aglow with lights, and the car park was jumping with cars and people.

'I'll park over here.' Neil manoeuvred the car to a spot where they wouldn't get blocked in.

Neil jumped out and went round to the passenger side to open her door, offering her a steady hand.

'I think I'll leave my coat in the car,' she said. 'It'll be easier when we want to leave or escape any trouble in a hurry.'

Neil smiled, helped her off with her coat and cast it on the back seat.

He was standing close to her now, too close, towering above her, causing her heart to react to him.

'Okay, Penny, let's go.' He clasped her hand, sending a shiver through her at his touch, and led her across the car park towards the front entrance of the castle. The doors were wide open and numerous couples and groups of people were arriving, all dressed to impress.

The energy was palpable. Lively Scottish music filtered out into the night air.

Penny looked around at the happy faces — the smiles, the laughter, the chatter as friends met up with each other, all commenting on how well they looked, teasing each other about their kilts and sporrans.

And that's when Penny started to relax. She felt Neil's reassuring and elegant fingers wrap around her hand, leading her inside the magnificent castle for an evening they would never forget.

Their first date.

Enjoy it, she told herself. Enjoy every minute. Dance your socks off.

She smiled up at Neil and he squeezed her hand.

'It sounds as if the live band have started playing,' he said. He'd checked the rundown of the evening on the castle's website. Live music, a delicious buffet and traditional dancing were included in the party night.

Walking in as a couple to the function room, they saw that the castle's hotel guests had already taken to the dance floor.

The ceilidh had begun. But the fireworks of friendly rivalry between Neil and Gaven hadn't yet kicked off. Gaven wasn't there.

Penny searched the faces for the tall, familiar laird and couldn't see him.

Etta, Robin and Aileen came hurrying over to Penny and Neil. The ladies were all wearing dresses, some with flashes of plaid or tartan sashes and low heel shoes for dancing.

'Gaven's not here yet.' Etta sounded concerned.

'I'm sure he'll turn up,' Neil assured her. He doubted Gaven would want to miss out on a chance to dance with Penny.

Jessy hurried over to join them. She was on duty, but dressed to join in some of the dancing.

'We can't find Gaven. He's not in his turret. He went there to get his kilt on, but no one has seen him since. Walter went hunting for him and he's disappeared too. If you see either of them, give me a shout.'

'We will,' Penny told Jessy.

'It's not like Gaven to shirk his duty as laird at a ceilidh night,' Aileen remarked.

'He's maybe delayed with a guest,' Neil suggested.

'Jessy had to announce the official start of the ceilidh so that the band could begin playing,' Etta told them. 'A lot of the hotel guests came down from their rooms early.'

In the far corner of the function room, a live band played traditional Scottish dance songs, filling the air with their lively music. A fire burned in the large fireplace, and buffet tables along one side of the room were laden with a feast for the guests.

'We're heading over to the buffet,' said Etta. 'None of us had any dinner so we could enjoy the food.

The castle's head chef, hat at a panicked tilt again, scuttled past them. 'I've made extra haggis vol–au–vents, Etta, so you won't be short changed at tonight's party.'

'Thank you,' Etta called to him as he sprinted on towards the buffet tables with a tray piled with mashed tattie and cheddar pies.

'Do you want to get something to eat before we hit the dance floor?' Neil said to Penny.

She hadn't eaten anything proper since her porridge breakfast. The day had tore in, and apart from cups of tea and a salad sandwich, she'd sewn all day and then ran around getting ready for the party.

'Yes, let's do that,' she said.

Penny let herself be escorted over to the buffet. Terrines of vegetables, including those filled with neeps and tatties, were set up along with smoked salmon sandwiches, and various savoury treats including sausage rolls and cheese pastries. Bowls of salad were alongside mini quiche. Cakes galore were on stands, including traditional Victoria sponge and Dundee cake. Large bowls were filled with trifle — and raspberry cranachan.

Neil and Penny both opted for a plate of neeps and tatties. Neil had haggis and gravy with his, while Penny wanted a Scottish cheddar pastry with tomato and bramble pickle. For pudding, Neil had traditional cranachan made with raspberries, oats and cream. Penny selected the strawberry trifle topped with a generous layer of whipped cream.

They sat at a table for two to enjoy their food.

Walter ran past them, took the racing line across the dance floor and headed over to Jessy. She was having something to eat along with Etta, Robin and Aileen. Sylvia and Aunt Muira were there too.

'Walter looks like he's in a tizzy,' Penny remarked.

Neil glanced around. 'There's still no sign of Gaven.'

They watched Walter's arms flapping as he explained whatever the predicament was. Jessy looked concerned, but Etta and the others seemed to be trying not to laugh.

Walter then ran back the way he came, dashing past Penny and Neil again. He disappeared out of the function room.

The lively music and dancing didn't falter, and party guests continued to link arms for one of the reels.

'Etta's coming over,' Penny said to Neil. 'We'll find out what's happened.'

'Gaven's got himself into a pickle,' Etta started to explain.

'Will he be joining us for the ceilidh?' Neil asked her.

'Yes, but he's upstairs in one of the empty guest rooms,' said Etta. 'He's scrubbing the verdigris off his bahookie.'

Penny laughed. 'He's what?'

'Gaven's a silly sausage,' Etta began. 'He thought he'd wear one of the castle's suits of armour to make an entrance for the start of the ceilidh, and then change into his kilt.' She shook her head. 'He took the armour up to his turret, put it on, but then he couldn't navigate his way down the turret's winding stairs. Not with the armour on. It wouldn't bend.'

'So what did he do?' Neil asked, intrigued.

'He tried to take two steps at a time so he could manoeuvre better,' Etta explained. 'But he took a tumble and bent his screws. He couldn't get the armour back off and had to phone Walter to come and rescue him.'

Penny and Neil laughed.

Etta tried to stifle a giggle. 'Walter had to use a pair of pliers to free Gaven from the suit of armour. But he's covered in green marks from wearing it. So he went into the guest bedroom to shower. It's got a fancy, high–powered shower. Walter has left him to it. Apparently, Gaven is using a loofah on his bahookie to get the marks off so he can wear his kilt and go commando.'

Neil couldn't eat his cranachan for laughing. 'I'm sorry, Etta. I shouldn't make fun of Gaven.'

Penny couldn't stop giggling.

'Shhh!' Etta said, suddenly seeing Gaven walk into the function room, looking dapper in his kilt and sporran. He wore a buttoned up shirt and tie with a waistcoat. 'Pretend we know nothing.' Etta then hurried back to join the other ladies.

Gaven's stride had a confident swagger, but as he walked past Penny, smiling at her, he noticed that Neil was wearing a ghillie shirt. From Gaven's expression, he looked like he wished he'd worn a lace up shirt. Nothing was going according to plan for him, including his hope of dancing with Penny. Neil had scuttled that.

Pretending he hadn't been thwarted from spending time with Penny, Gaven continued on, greeting guests and playing the gracious host.

Walter came scurrying back in, and went over to talk to Jessy.

'I've a feeling it's going to be an extra wild night this evening,' said Neil.

Penny agreed. 'Remember, if we need to make a run for it, my coat is in the car.'

Neil stood up and offered Penny his hand. 'Come on, let's join in the next reel.'

'Is it one of the dances we practiced?' she asked hopefully.

'No, but you can handle it,' he assured her. 'Hold tight to my hand and I'll keep you right.'

Penny let Neil lead her on to the dance floor as the band started to play a lively tune for the fast–moving reel.

To her left was Neil, and to her right was Fyn, and he was holding hands with Aileen. Fyn suited wearing his kilt and open neck shirt.

'Are you enjoying yourself, Penny?' said Fyn.

'Ask me after this reel,' Penny said, sounding anxious.

Fyn smiled to her and nodded acknowledgement to Neil.

Neil smiled at Fyn, and then the dance kicked off to the lively music.

Penny let herself enjoy the fast–pace of the dance, trying not to mess up the rhythm, but soon she was smiling and loving the exhilarating feeling.

The reel then became another dance, and Neil and Penny continued to join in, dancing, laughing, twirling and skip–stepping to the music.

It was a night to remember — filled with dancing, great music, delicious food and the company of friends.

A couple of prestigious and very attractive women, waylaid Gaven, and as they were guests at the castle, he was happy to give them his time and attention.

There was one brief moment when Neil had gone to get soft refreshments from the bar, leaving Penny sitting at a table watching the antics on the dance floor.

Gaven approached Penny. 'Can I have this dance?' He extended his hand to her.

Feeling she couldn't refuse without causing friction, Penny glanced at Neil, queuing at the busy bar, and then took Gaven's hand.

The laird's kilt had an extra swagger to it as he took Penny in his arms for a slower, waltz style dance. He led her around the dance floor, circling past Etta, Jessy and other members of the bee.

Penny saw Etta nudge Jessy as she waltzed by.

Sylvia was up dancing with one of the strapping farmers, as was Aileen.

Fyn and Oliver were dancing with ladies that Penny didn't recognise, others from the community or guests, she didn't know.

Oliver wore a kilt with a dark shirt and dark waistcoat. He cut a dramatic figure, and he smiled to her as they danced past each other.

Bradoch was there too, kilted and wearing a white ghillie shirt but no waistcoat. Penny hadn't seen him dance yet with Sylvia, but Bradoch wasn't short of ladies willing to whirl around in the arms of the kilted baker.

'Have you been to many ceilidh nights?' Gaven asked Penny as they waltzed around the floor.

'A few, but never in a castle, only in hotel function rooms,' Penny told him.

They were going to continue chatting, but the music changed, and as people got ready for the next dance, Neil stepped in and reclaimed Penny.

'May I have the next dance, Penny?' Neil said politely, but in a tone that left Gaven in no doubt that she was his lady.

Penny was glad to be back in Neil's arms.

Gaven forced a resigned smile, and then walked away.

'I'm sorry,' said Neil. 'The bar was so busy.'

'It's fine,' Penny assured him. 'It would've looked strange if I hadn't danced with the laird.'

Neil pulled her close. 'I'm going to claim the rest of the night's dances, if that's okay with you.'

Penny smiled up at him and nodded.

Neil and Penny waltzed around until the next lively reel when they joined in with the fun.

As the evening wore on, it was clear to everyone that Penny and Neil were a couple, and although they joined in the reels and jigs, they only had eyes for each other.

When Penny had danced with Gaven, she acknowledged he was handsome. There was no doubt about that. But even when he held her in his arms and she waltzed with him, Gaven didn't make her feel the way she did about Neil.

Throughout the evening, her heart ached and fluttered and was filled with happiness in Neil's company. The question she'd asked herself earlier in the night, if she was Neil's girlfriend, was answered clearly, without a word being spoken. She was Neil's girlfriend all right. And she felt her heart fill with joy and contentment — and excitement. The perfect mix, she thought. Neil was the perfect man for her.

Oliver looked anxious as he finally plucked up the nerve to approach Robin. She was standing at the buffet, deciding what to have when he walked up to her.

'I wondered if you'd like to dance with me,' Oliver said to her.

He'd long admired her. He'd heard that she was dating one of the farmers, and hadn't made a move to ask her out. The rumour of a romance with a farmer wasn't true, so now he felt he could approach her.

'I was going to have something to eat,' Robin said to Oliver. 'I've been dancing all evening, but...' She put her empty plate down and smiled at him. 'Okay.'

Oliver's heart thundered in his broad chest as he took Robin in his arms and danced with her. This was their first dance. It was a start, he thought hopefully, seeing her lovely face smile at him as they waltzed together.

After midnight, people started to filter out, while others stayed to continue dancing.

Neil and Penny bid their friends goodnight, and then stepped out into the cold evening air.

Neil wrapped his arm around Penny's shoulders and hurried her to the car.

'Come on. I'll heat the car up.'

He helped her on with her coat, then she sat in the passenger seat as Neil started up the engine and turned the heater up.

He drove them off, away from the castle.

Penny glanced back at the castle, still aglow with lights and activity. 'I had a great night, Neil.'

He smiled over at her. 'So did I.'

As he drove away from the castle, he glanced out the window. It was a cold but dry and clear night.

'Are you tired?' Neil said to her. 'Do you want me to take you straight back to your cottage?'

'What else did you have in mind?'

'It's such a fine evening. We could take the scenic route home, enjoy the view from the hilltop without it raining. Evenings like this feel great. The view is amazing.'

'I'm sold on the idea.' Penny relaxed back in her seat.

Neil smiled and headed up to the hillside road.

The higher up they drove, the better the view. Penny peered out the passenger side window. 'I can see the lights from the castle way over there.'

'Wait until you see the miles of countryside from the top.'

A rush of excitement charged through her. She loved the feeling of being out late at night, in the beautiful Scottish Highlands. And it was right on her doorstep.

Neil parked the car where they'd stopped the last time.

Penny smiled to herself. This was the local kissing spot, but no way was she reminding Neil of this.

Neil gestured to the vast view of the fields and countryside. 'I love this view.'

'I can see lights glittering in the distance. That must be from some of the farmhouses.'

'It is, and cottages.'

Penny looked at Neil, thinking how handsome he looked. There were a fair few handsome men at the ceilidh, but only one of them made her heart melt and ache to be with him. And that was Neil.

The laces on his shirt front had become undone, revealing his strong, smooth chest that she yearned to run her hands over. She was supposed to be admiring the view, and she was, the one outside the car and the one sitting next to her.

Neil wanted to tell Penny that he'd fallen in love with her, that he wanted them to make a future together here in the Scottish Highlands. Should he tell her now, or wait until they'd had another couple of dates? He wasn't sure, but one thing he was certain of and that was the depths of his feelings for Penny. He'd never felt like this before. She was the one for him.

'You're looking very serious, thinking deep thoughts,' she said lightly.

He gazed at her with those gorgeous blue eyes and nodded. 'I am. I'm wondering whether to tell you that I love you, or wait until we've dated a few times.'

Her heart soared, but she smiled at him. 'Difficult decision. I'm not sure whether to tell you that I feel the same way.'

Neil gently pulled her close to him and smiled warmly. 'I didn't know that this was known as the kissing spot when I first brought you here.'

'I believe you.'

'But now that we're here...' he leaned over and kissed her.

She kissed his firm, sensual lips, and then smiled at him. It was a night to remember, she thought. She would remember their first date at the ceilidh, and their first kiss here.

He kissed her again, and she ran her hands over his chest, feeling the muscles beneath her fingers and the strong beating of his heart.

They cuddled up and gazed out at the magnificent view. The inky dark sky arched all around them, and the vast countryside stretched into the distance. Penny could see her future here with Neil. A happy future together in the heart of the Highlands.

End

About the Author:

De-ann Black is a bestselling author, scriptwriter and former newspaper journalist. She has over 100 books published. Romance, thrillers, espionage novels, action adventure. And children's books (non-fiction rocket science books and children's fiction). She became an Amazon All-Star author in 2014 and 2015.

She previously worked as a full-time newspaper journalist for several years. She had her own weekly columns in the press. This included being a motoring correspondent where she got to test drive cars every week for the press for three years.

Before being asked to work for the press, De-ann worked in magazine editorial writing everything from fashion features to social news. She was the marketing editor of a glossy magazine.

She is also a professional artist and illustrator. Embroidery design, fabric design, dressmaking, sewing, knitting and fashion are part of her work.

Additionally, De-ann has always been interested in fitness, and was a fitness and bodybuilding champion, 100 metre runner and mountaineer. As a former N.A.B.B.A. Miss Scotland, she had a weekly fitness show on the radio that ran for over three years.

De-ann trained in Shukokai karate, boxing, kickboxing, Dayan Qigong and Jiu Jitsu. She is currently based in Scotland.

Her 16 colouring books are available in paperback, including her latest Summer Nature Colouring Book and Flower Nature Colouring Book.

Her latest embroidery pattern books include: Floral Garden Embroidery Patterns, Christmas & Winter Embroidery Patterns, Floral Spring Embroidery Patterns and Sea Theme Embroidery Patterns.

Website: Find out more at: www.de-annblack.com

Fabric, Wallpaper & Home Decor Collections:
De-ann's fabric designs and wallpaper collections, and home decor items, including her popular Scottish Garden Thistles patterns, are available from Spoonflower.
www.de-annblack.com/spoonflower

Also by De-ann Black (Romance, Action/Thrillers & Children's books). See her Amazon Author page or website for further details about her books, screenplays, illustrations, art, fabric designs and embroidery patterns.

Amazon Author page:
www.De-annBlack.com/Amazon

Romance books:

Snow Bells Haven series:
1. Snow Bells Christmas
2. Snow Bells Wedding
3. Love & Lyrics

Scottish Highlands & Island Romance series:
1. Scottish Island Knitting Bee
2. Scottish Island Fairytale Castle
3. Vintage Dress Shop on the Island
4. Fairytale Christmas on the Island

Scottish Loch Romance series:
1. Sewing & Mending Cottage
2. Scottish Loch Summer Romance
3. Sweet Music

Quilting Bee & Tea Shop series:
1. The Quilting Bee
2. The Tea Shop by the Sea
3. Embroidery Cottage
4. Knitting Shop by the Sea
5. Christmas Weddings

Sewing, Crafts & Quilting series:
1. The Sewing Bee
2. The Sewing Shop
3. Knitting Cottage (Scottish Highland romance)
4. Scottish Highlands Christmas Wedding

The Cure for Love Romance series:
1. The Cure for Love
2. The Cure for Love at Christmas

Cottages, Cakes & Crafts series:
1. The Flower Hunter's Cottage
2. The Sewing Bee by the Sea
3. The Beemaster's Cottage
4. The Chocolatier's Cottage
5. The Bookshop by the Seaside
6. The Dressmaker's Cottage

Scottish Chateau, Colouring & Crafts series:
1. Christmas Cake Chateau
2. Colouring Book Cottage

Summer Sewing Bee

Sewing, Knitting & Baking series:
1. The Tea Shop
2. The Sewing Bee & Afternoon Tea
3. The Christmas Knitting Bee
4. Champagne Chic Lemonade Money
5. The Vintage Sewing & Knitting Bee

Tea Dress Shop series:
1. The Tea Dress Shop At Christmas
2. The Fairytale Tea Dress Shop In Edinburgh
3. The Vintage Tea Dress Shop In Summer

The Tea Shop & Tearoom series:
1. The Christmas Tea Shop & Bakery
2. The Christmas Chocolatier
3. The Chocolate Cake Shop in New York at Christmas
4. The Bakery by the Seaside
5. Shed in the City

Christmas Romance series:
1. Christmas Romance in Paris
2. Christmas Romance in Scotland

Oops! I'm the Paparazzi series:
1. Oops! I'm the Paparazzi
2. Oops! I'm Up To Mischief
3. Oops! I'm the Paparazzi, Again

The Bitch-Proof Suit series:
1. The Bitch-Proof Suit
2. The Bitch-Proof Romance
3. The Bitch-Proof Bride
4. The Bitch-Proof Wedding

Heather Park: Regency Romance
Dublin Girl
Why Are All The Good Guys Total Monsters?
I'm Holding Out For A Vampire Boyfriend

Action/Thriller books:

Knight in Miami
Agency Agenda
Love Him Forever
Someone Worse
Electric Shadows
The Strife Of Riley
Shadows Of Murder
Cast a Dark Shadow

Children's books:

Faeriefied
Secondhand Spooks
Poison-Wynd
Wormhole Wynd
Science Fashion
School For Aliens

Colouring books:

Summer Nature
Flower Nature
Summer Garden
Spring Garden
Autumn Garden
Sea Dream
Festive Christmas
Christmas Garden
Christmas Theme
Flower Bee
Wild Garden
Faerie Garden Spring
Flower Hunter
Stargazer Space
Bee Garden
Scottish Garden
Seasons

Embroidery Design books:

Sea Theme Embroidery Patterns
Floral Garden Embroidery Patterns
Christmas & Winter Embroidery Patterns
Floral Spring Embroidery Patterns
Floral Nature Embroidery Designs
Scottish Garden Embroidery Designs

Printed in Great Britain
by Amazon